She stretched her arms over her head and formed a triangle with her fingers. She closed her eyes and began to move her lips in a silent chant. She started to glow a bright green, and then the color of pure light. Opening her eyes, two rays of blinding brilliance shot out of them and into the triangle with a thundering sound.

Her back arched, her legs hunched, and a tail began to grow from her spine. Her hands balled as the fingers receded into the palms. The nails became claws. Soft brown fur began to grow on the naked animal that stood in the center of the light. Then she was gone. In her place stood a shiny, brown cat the size of a panther.

Hatisha clapped her hands. "Oh, but I do admire the work of a true artist!"

The cat's tail swished irritably.

THE BRENTWOOD WITCHES

BRENDA JORDAN

ACE BOOKS, NEW YORK

This book is an Ace
original edition, and has never
been previously published.

THE BRENTWOOD WITCHES

An Ace Book / published by arrangement with
the author

PRINTING HISTORY
Ace edition / October 1987

ISBN: 0-441-07297-6

Ace Books are published by
The Berkley Publishing Group,
200 Madison Avenue, New York, New York 10016.

PRINTED IN THE UNITED STATES OF AMERICA

10 9 8 7 6 5 4 3 2 1

1

The Brentwood hockey fans bolted straight up from their stadium seats as Jesse Trent scored his fifth goal of the game. Teammates slapped his back and shoulders as the crowd screamed wildly. It was the Brentwood High School alumni against the alumni from Hoopersville. Jesse had wondered if the reason so many came to the exhibition game was to escape the hot autumn weather rather than to see the game itself, but the cheers now suggested otherwise.

It was great to be home. College just wasn't what he had expected. He was lonely without his hometown, the people he knew, his parents—without *her*. If it hadn't been for her weekly visits, he was sure he wouldn't have survived this long. The ice moved easily under his skates as they reassembled for the next charge. Hoopersville moved the puck down the ice, determined not to remain scoreless.

Larry Caylin maneuvered the puck carefully with his stick as he watched Jesse closely. He hated Jesse. All the girls from Brentwood and Hoopersville talked about him as though he were the only male alive. He was tall, handsome, smart, and too damned good at everything. Larry moved and dipped to his left as he skated across the rink. His wings took out several Brentwood alumni as Larry bore down on the Brentwood goalie knowing the guy favored his left side. With his best friend, Bobby Mayfield, guarding his own right, Larry was assured of scoring. As if in a dream, Jesse appeared out of nowhere and with a liquid movement he intercepted the puck from Larry and sent it sailing down the ice to a teammate.

"Damn you!" Larry muttered under his breath, and before he realized what he was doing, he body-checked Jesse into the rink wall. Fists flew and bodies entangled. Both teams rushed to pull the two star players apart. Jesse calmed down immediately but Larry still had to be restrained. The look of amusement on Jesse's face only served to provoke him further. As he struggled futilely, Bobby's voice rang clearly in his ear.

"What are you doing? Are you crazy? Remember who that is!"

The referee blew his whistle and skated back toward the center of the ice. Everyone relaxed and returned to their positions. Bobby let go of Larry.

"You're nuts, man!" He skated away shaking his head.

Picking up his stick, Larry threw a look in Jesse's direction before heading to the penalty box. Unruffled, not a hair out of place, thought Larry, disgusted. He wiped at the small cut on his lip. Maybe what everyone whispered about Jesse was true. . . .

Jonathan Webster wiped the dirt from his hands as he walked from his cornfield. The report was true. There would be no corn this harvest. The fertilizer had been mixed wrong at the factory, with too much of the chemical Biuret, which killed the seed in the ground. Every farmer in town had planted with it. Instead of stalks ready for harvest, there were miles of empty fields. Jonathan removed his hat and wiped its inner rim with his handkerchief. There was only one thing to do. Replacing his hat, he headed for the truck.

Mary glanced over her shoulder at her husband. He had made the decision, she could tell by his walk. After twenty-seven years, his walk told her everything. She dropped the sheet from the line into the wicker basket and removed the pillowcase from her shoulder. Holding it in her hands she twisted and untwisted it as she moved toward him.

Jonathan opened the door of the primer-colored truck and paused. He looked into her green eyes, searching for the coolness that relaxed him. He loved her so much. She had been the only one in the town who hadn't treated him differently after he had been appointed by Hatisha. She stopped twisting the pillowcase and folded it carefully, avoiding his eyes.

"What will we do now?" she asked, looking up.

"Hatisha." His voice was emotionless. Mary's expression tightened. He shrugged.

"It has to be."

With that said, he climbed into the truck and drove away. Mary carried the pillowcase to the basket and dropped it in. She watched the dust from Jonathan's truck billowing up beneath the tailgate and she worried, as she always worried, every time he went to her.

The steam drifted among the men in the showers as they snapped towels at one another. The laughter in the locker room rose and fell with each new joke or gag. Jesse pulled up his jeans and fastened them. He felt strong and sleek, like an animal. He was sure he could actually feel his blood coursing through his veins, a thought he found powerfully stimulating. His thoughts turned to Tamara. Had there ever been a time when he hadn't thought of her? He knew there must have been, but he couldn't imagine it. She had always been there, as far back as he could remember, though it wasn't until his sixteenth birthday that she had offered him eternity. . . .

Jesse realized that the room had grown quiet. He reached slowly, casually, into his locker and withdrew his shirt. Pulling it over his head, he tried to sense the exact location of the enemy. His muscles were tight with readiness. His senses tingled with anticipation. It was hard to keep the faintest smile from penetrating his neutral expression.

"It's not natural. Nobody plays the way you do. Nobody can be that good at everything he does. Not unless—"

"What's the matter, Caylin," interrupted Jesse without turning around, "did you bruise your ego as well as your lip?" He ran his fingers through his dark, wet hair with an easy gesture.

It made Larry angry that Jesse refused to turn and face him. His anger urged him closer to Jesse, but not too close. Bobby reached out from the crowd that was gathering around the two and tried to grab Larry's arm, but Larry jerked it away.

"Everyone's afraid of you—but I'm not. I say it's time we found out about you."

"Larry!" pleaded Bobby.

Brentwood's men gathered close by Jesse and stood their ground. Larry looked at each face, searching for fear. He found none. Why did they protect Jesse? How could they be on Jesse's side? Maybe they were under the same spell. But then, not even Larry's best friend Bobby would stand with him. Jesse stepped forward. His six-foot frame matched Larry's height, but he still seemed to tower above him.

"Sports have always been easy for me. After all the years you and I have competed, you should know that. I don't need help from anyone or anything. If you can't take the heat of the game, Caylin, then get out."

Jesse returned to the inside of his locker and retrieved his watch from the shelf. Everyone began moving away, and the chatter and laughter returned. Larry felt mortified. He had been dismissed. He wanted to attack Jesse again. To smash him with his fists until his pretty face wasn't pretty anymore. But Bobby pulled at his arm, and Larry allowed himself to be led out of the locker room into the tunnel that rose up to the exit doors.

"I just don't believe you sometimes! Where do you put your brain when you're not usin' it? You've gotta be crazy or somethin', confrontin' him like that!" Bobby shivered.

"He doesn't scare me!" Larry fumed, slamming his fist against the tunnel wall. Bobby moved up behind him and leaned closer to Larry's ear to whisper.

"Then you'd better be afraid of *her*. *She's* the one you should worry about!"

"Pull into the next station, I'm dying for a drink!" Paul shifted his position, searching for comfort. "How I ever let you talk me into this, I'll never know! I could be skinny-dipping in my pool with luscious Nancy Beck right at this moment. But no!" He threw a look at Richard, who was grinning from ear to ear. "What's so funny?"

"You."

"Me?"

"Yeah. Do you know that you haven't stopped bitching since we left?" Richard wiped at his sweating face with his arm.

"If you knew Nancy, you'd be bitching too!" Paul banged on the air conditioner. "Why isn't it cooler in here? What's wrong with this damn thing?"

"Witches' Eve," Richard replied as he changed lanes on the empty highway.

"Witches' Eve! That's all you've been talking about ever since we ran across that nutso on our last video feature."

"Phillip Jesoppe is an author, not a nutso."

"The guy is a fruitcake! Witches, goblins and ghosties, things that go bump in the night!" Paul rose out of his seat, arms arched like huge claws, his teeth faking vampire fangs as he leaned toward Richard.

"Cut it out, ya want us to hit somebody!" Richard laughed as he switched hands on the steering wheel and adjusted the rearview mirror.

"Who's to hit? I haven't seen another living soul for miles!" Paul moaned as he collapsed back into his seat. "How you ever talked our producer into this scheme is beyond me. Hey! Now there's some magic, right there! And we wouldn't have had to leave home! Talking Nate into this scheme was definitely a feat of witchcraft. Ol' state Nate. The ogre of budget-cutters. Imagine him, shelling out money so you can get over your homesickness!"

"I'm not homesick. You're just tired."

"You betcha! Running around by car in the Midwest is *not* my idea of a good time."

"Listen, when we get to Brentwood, I'll buy you a big steak dinner. We'll get a room, you can watch some TV and relax." Richard looked over for a reaction. Paul's eyes were closed and his fingers were interlaced on his chest.

"Relax? In a town you claim is full of witches? Make up your mind, Rich!"

Richard sighed. It was a good thing that he and Paul were good friends because sometimes Richard felt like slugging him. Paul was one of the best damned photojournalists Richard had ever met. That, combined with Paul's sense of humor and penchant for getting into trouble, had caused Richard to like him immediately. Their friendship and devotion to each other often led people to assume they were brothers, despite the fact that Paul was five-eight, thin and wiry, with light brown hair and quick eyes, and Richard had black hair, was six-foot-one and owned a body that only hard work, determination and Nautilus could create. His dark eyes were thoughtful and easy to trust.

The two men had seen Vietnam, Columbia, South Africa, Israel—anywhere it was hot, that's where they went. The two youngest guys in the business, and they had racked up enough awards to fill a room. And on this trip, if everything went well, he and Paul would be up to their necks in the biggest supernatural story of all time. Richard spotted a station up ahead.

"Everything Phillip Jesoppe said made sense to me, because it happened in this town when I was a kid," he said once again to Paul. He spotted a gas station at last.

"Yeah, sure." Paul's eyes stayed closed. "You told me you were just a little guy when you moved; how can you remember anything accurately?"

"Jesoppe's book reminded me. Once I read it, everything fell into place. He said that the witches needed the protection of local communities to keep from being detected. That's how many of the witches survived the local witch hunts."

"Witch hunts." Paul swatted away a fly as he sat up. "And what did these local communities get in return for all this protection? Free broom rides on Halloween?"

"In return, the witches would see to it the harvest was always good so that the towns would never go hungry."

"Well, either your witches are dead or they're fallin' down on the job, because all I see are empty fields and this is supposed to be the harvest, right, ploughboy?"

Richard pulled into the gas station and parked. The two of them got out of the car into the heat and stood at the edge of the field, which was barren, although this should have been harvest time.

"Well, Rich," began Paul as he headed for the soft drink machine, "all I gotta say is there better be some excitement in your town this weekend, or we'll have to head home via Las Vegas to make up for me missing Nancy."

"There'll be plenty of action," Richard promised. Come Witches' Eve, he added to himself.

• • •

Jonathan brought the truck to a stop in front of a beautiful, ancient, three-story house. It was the only one of its kind in Brentwood, with gabled roofs, carved window ledges, and two spire towers. The bay windows were large, with arching tops and marvelous flower boxes, each filled with bright blooms, despite the heat. Jonathan sat quietly, watching the house. He always felt nervous around it, though he never outwardly showed it to others. His thoughts wandered back to his childhood.

He and the other children had always walked the other side of the street when passing the house; no one even wanted to play near it. Not until the night of the dare. Jonathan and his friends had slept over at Billy's house. They had waited for Billy's parents to fall asleep so the group could sneak out, then they had stolen quietly to the bushes surrounding the old house and peered at it through the leaves. In the warm night, lit only by the moon, the house's windows seemed to be menacing eyes.

They had drawn straws, and Jonathan had come up short. So he tried the front door and found it open. Looking back to his friends, he hoped that they had fled so that he could follow suit, but they were still in the bushes waving him in. The door creaked and moaned as it opened into the house. Jonathan's heart pounded in his throat as he peered into the darkness. He eased across the threshold, putting his back against the inside wall as his hand remained on the exterior doorknob. His eyes darted around, looking for anything that might move, but they had not yet adjusted to the darkness. It was time to close the door, but Jonathan was frozen where he stood as if holding on to the doorknob was his link to the outside world. It was the hardest thing he had ever done in his life but somehow he found the strength to close the door, the light from the moon vanishing to the sound of the clicking lock. Trembling, Jonathan grasped the front of his shirt in his hands as if he were pulling himself forward. He could make out a stairway to his right and some sort of furnishings to his left, but his eyes were busy searching for monsters. He fumbled in the darkness, trying not to put anything between himself and his path to the door. Then he sat down on the floor and drew his knees to his chin and hugged himself with his arms. He thought he heard sounds above him and searched the ceiling in the darkness. The thought of bats hanging upside down from the rafters ready to strike was all his young mind could take. It was time to leave, he decided. It felt as if he had already spent a lifetime validating his courage; he began to move toward the door.

"Jonathan Webster!" Her words shattered the stillness like glass. He froze. His heart pounded savagely. He couldn't breath as he turned his head to look across the room at the rocking chair by the hearth. Two crystal-blue eyeballs stared back at him. He could see nothing but the eyes in the darkness.

Getting out of the truck, Jonathan closed its door quietly, almost reverently. He moved up the walk to the front door and let himself in, knowing the door would be unlocked. After all, what did *she* have to fear?

Jesse slammed the locker closed. With graceful ease he swung his backpack over his shoulder and walked to the door. As he touched the handle, a soft voice sang in his ear. He grinned and quickly turned, searching for her. The room was empty. Slowly, he lowered the pack to the floor as he joined in the game, moving catlike toward the first row of lockers. He peered carefully around the row and moved on to the next when he found nothing. The farther down he moved, the less he felt her presence, so he returned to the first two rows. His eyes settled on a locker and he quickly pulled it open, but he found it empty. Another locker. Empty. His smile faded with his patience, and he called to her.

"Tamara?"

Her silent laugh made the hair on his neck stand up, and Jesse realized that he had forgotten a very important lesson. He stopped and stood rigid as steel, clearing his mind of everything, his hands held up in front of him like searching radar. Then, he felt it. A disturbance in the energy around him. Tamara had taught him many things these past two years, but one of the most important was how to use his natural senses. His grin returned and he leaped into the shower. Empty.

"Tamara!" he called urgently, wanting the game to end. She touched his shoulder, sliding seductively around his body to his front. He quickly sought her lips, wanting all of her. She withdrew slowly, smiling, her dark eyes dancing with laughter.

"You're getting better," she said softly. "You almost caught me!"

He pulled her close again, his hands sliding down her hips. Burying his face in her dark hair, he inhaled her fragrance. She played with the back of his neck, lightly scratching it with her nails, before her fingers roamed into his hair. He felt drunk with her closeness. It was always this way with her. Always this want. This need. He had to have her.

"You played magnificently tonight."

"You were at the game?" Jesse asked as he pulled her to the shower floor.

"No." She smiled.

Hatisha's ancient fingers roamed through her herbs. Sacramelia, Heatherspent, Taferand, Megas and Fore. Magic herbs, grown over the centuries by Hatisha's wisdom and care. She selected some Megas, picking it up carefully between gnarled fingers. Blowing on it to stir its aroma, she dropped it into a quarter-size clay pot. Hatisha sniffed it once more before closing the lid. She loved its smell, for it reminded her of violets.

She sensed his arrival, her inner eye watching the primer-colored truck pull up in front. She smiled. After all these years, he was still hesitant about approaching her. After all her kindness. She replaced the lid on the wooden herb box and stretched up her arm to put the herbs above the stove, but her bent spine wouldn't permit it. She grumbled obscenities and tottered across the kitchen floor. Stopping, she looked back over her shoulder at the exact place she wanted the box to be on the shelf, her crystal-blue eyes beginning to glow. As they became blinding, a radiance shot out of her eyes to the shelf. The box disappeared from her hand and reappeared in its proper place. Hatisha chuckled merrily to herself, feeling smug. He was in the living room now. Her eyes returned to their ice-blueness; mustn't scare him away, she thought to herself.

In here, she said with her mind. Jonathan felt her words, and a chill ran up his spine. As he entered the kitchen, he saw her slip the tightly capped clay pot into her robe pocket. He held back, waiting for her to speak. Mortals were not permitted to speak first.

"I understand there is a problem with the corn for this harvest?"

"Yes, Hatisha. The whole town is affected. I waited until now to come to you because I wanted to be sure. I know you don't like to be disturbed."

"Humph!" croaked Hatisha. "That is a mortal notion. I suppose if you ran to me with every little problem I could become annoyed. But I've never had to put up with that from you, Jonathan. You've been my favorite."

Jonathan felt himself blushing. It was unlike her to be so free with compliments. It was then he remembered his hat and quickly removed it, so as not to displease her. Her lips lifted into a smile at his gesture. She would have to be very displeased indeed to ever hurt Jonathan. She recalled how, when he was a small boy, she had levitated him off the floor and transported him to the couch after he had fainted. He had been the bravest child she had ever met. Brave, indeed, to have entered her house. A quiet child, he had been a perfect choice as replacement for her speaker—a go-between when the town wanted something or she wanted a message delivered. The speaker at the time had been Benton Russell, but he died of old age and Hatisha didn't mind seeing him go. He was always terrified of Hatisha, well into his nineties, and it wasn't as if he hadn't lived within his mortal time span. But Jonathan had been a joy. He had accepted the job without comment, kept to himself, and didn't whisper about "the witch" whenever he gathered with friends. Hatisha hated mortal gossips. Their fears always led them to fabricating the palest account of witch-doings into wild, colorful orgies of baby-eating and spell-casting.

"It will be taken care of." Hatisha put her teakettle on the fire, rather than conjuring it up in the usual way. She didn't need to show off. Besides, she knew it made Jonathan nervous. Magic always made mortals nervous.

"Thank you." He bowed slightly, turning to leave.

"No. Don't go, stay," encouraged Hatisha as she moved

easily about her kitchen, despite her back. Her lips moved in silent chant as she made her tea. Jonathan watched the hunched form and wondered why she looked so old and yet the other witches were young, beautiful women. She looked like the stereotypical Halloween witch, from her aged wrinkled face, hooked nose, and gnarled hands to her long, silver-gray hair. Everything associated with how a witch would look—except there were no warts on her nose! Hatisha finished her chanting and stirred her tea. This was the first time he had wondered about her in her presence. She owed him this one.

"I used to be beautiful, like a spring day," she croaked. "But some time ago, I underestimated a foe and engaged in combat. The encounter stole my powers of youth." She winked at him. "But I have yet to give up every pleasure!" She laughed a deep, throaty laugh. "Go home, Jonathan. Do not fear, all is well." She took her tea to the table and sat down.

"Thank you, thank you, Hatisha," he managed haltingly, and hurried out of the house.

The old woman let her inner eye wander. She found Tamara and Jesse on a grassy hill just outside of town. Hatisha smiled.

Tamara felt the inner touch and smiled back. She knew Hatisha was only curious, nothing was wrong. She returned the feeling of love.

Jesse stirred in Tamara's arms. They were both dressed, but Jesse was shirtless. He turned to his back and rubbed his face with his hands. Tamara was leaning against a wide tree trunk, with Jesse using her lap for his pillow. She looked down the hill, watching the town of Brentwood. Jesse stretched his arms up behind him to touch her face as he lay with his eyes closed. She bit his fingers gently, holding them in her mouth. He opened his eyes and looked up at her with a grin. She smiled back and kissed his fingers. His face grew serious as he turned around and looked deeply into her eyes.

"Take me on the Eve." Her look wandered away from his to the town, and it was several seconds before she answered, her face devoid of any emotion.

"No."

"Please, Tamara, I don't want to wait."

"You must." She brushed the hair at his forehead without looking down. Her tone was quiet and patient.

"I can't go back to college." He sulked.

"School is important. Knowledge is power. Power is survival. You must learn to survive," she said as though reciting a lesson.

"I'm lonely there." He looked pleadingly at her.

"I come for you." Her gaze was still fixed on the town.

Once a week: He got up, brushed off his jeans and walked to another tree close by. With his back to her, he began plucking leaves off of the tree and examining them one by one.

"You must stay in school."

"Why?" His voice had an edge as he turned.

"Because, afterward you won't, and uneducated men bore me." She smiled at him, her dark eyes measuring his mood.

"Afterward I won't need to. I'll have anything I desire."

Her smile left her and she returned her attention to the town. He swallowed with difficulty. Had he made her angry? He knew he was treading dangerous ground. To question a witch was to invite trouble. He had displeased her only once before, by taking another lover. She had made sure he regretted that. He drew a breath. Turning, he put his hands on his hips in an easy gesture, rather than a hostile one.

"Tamara, I'm not going back to school. You can punish me if you want, but I won't change my mind. You said you loved me. Well, if that's true, prove it. Perform the ceremony on Witches' Eve."

She was silent, never taking her eyes from the town as she rose up from her place by the tree. Had he gone too far?

She walked a few feet away, staring down into the town. Her eyes began to glow.

"What is it?" Jesse asked as he tried to sense what was going on.

"I must go."

Jesse returned to the tree and retrieved his shirt. When he turned, just a moment later, she'd vanished. "Damn it!" he moaned. Now he had to walk home. He was two miles out of town and it was eighty-nine degrees in the shade. He threw the shirt over his shoulder and descended the hill.

● ● ●

ain't ya?"

The woman on the landing wore black, like the other woman, only this one was blond and not as shapely.

"Do you think maybe now you could find us a room?"

The woman on the landing silently moved up the stairs and out of Paul's view.

"Well, you're not exactly a stranger anymore. Maybe." His look wandered to Paul, who was about to climb the stairs. "What about him?" Feeders' eyebrows arched in speculation.

"Him?" asked Richard, jabbing a thumb in Paul's direction. Feeders nodded. "Oh, he's alright. He hallucinates once in a while, but he's harmless," kidded Richard. His remark caused Paul to turn.

"Who is that woman?" he asked, gesturing to the stairs.

"I see what ya mean," said Jethro. He turned to the mailboxes beside him and extracted a key. "Ain't nobody up there, 'til we get up there." He trudged up the stairs with ease. "Follow me."

Paul grabbed Richard's arm as they went. "What do you mean, harmless?"

Jethro opened the door to their room and let them enter before him. "No one else is visitin' right now, so the missus don't lay out no fancy spread. But you're welcome to take your meals with us or at the diner down the street, if ya like."

"Don't go to any trouble for us. We'll be in and out, so we'll eat at the diner."

"Well, then, here's your key." Handing it over, he gave Paul the once-over before heading out the door. He paused. "Jes' what are you boys doing here, this time of year?"

"Vacation. I wanted to show my friend where I used to live."

"Folks never come back—if they leave." He closed the door behind him.

"Are we talking weird, or what? God, Rich! It's no wonder you've got spooky memories of this place. That guy's S-T-R-A-N-G-E! And there *was* a woman on the stairs." Paul carefully opened the door and checked the hallway.

"Maybe it was Mrs. Feeders. Anyway, that guy was already an old man last time I saw him. He's got to be in his eighties or nineties by now and he doesn't even look like he qualifies for social security yet."

"Believe me, it wasn't the 'missus.' She was dressed just like the woman I saw out on the street, sort of old-fashioned."

"Now are you curious enough to stay and find out a little more?"

"Uncle, already!" Paul laughed, holding up his hands in surrender.

The two little boys burst out of the cornfield and continued their race past the town hall, the church, through the market square—practically upsetting a man with a wheel barrel full of bricks—down through the alley behind the bank, over an empty lot and around Mr. Heely's dry goods store. The best of friends, Tony and Willie were as different as night and day. Willie's dark curls bounced around his head as he pulled out just ahead of Tony.

"C'mon Red, I'm winnin'!" he teased, knowing how much Tony hated the nickname given to him because of his short, bright red hair. The joke worked too well, for it spurred Tony on as he moved out in front.

The finish line loomed ahead, an apple tree heavy with fruit, and each boy stretched and stretched for the last precious inches as they touched the tree at the same time. Willie collapsed on the ground trying to regain his breath while Tony leaned against the tree catching his. They realized they were both very much out of breath and each stole a look at the same time causing them to break out into peals of laughter. Tony slid down, his back against the tree trunk, until he was sitting. Willie crawled over and sat next to him.

"People must think we've lost our brains!"

"Runnin' in this heat?"

"Yep."

The two looked at one another. "Yep!" They giggled in unison. All giggled out, they were quiet for several moments as Willie stared up into the branches.

"I want an apple, I surely do."

"We done picked all we could reach." Tony looked up too.

"Maybe I could climb?"

"You always say that, when you know you can't!"

"I'm gettin' taller."

"Those apples'll be awful rotten by the time you're tall enough!"

Suddenly, the apples started falling from the tree, one by one, at first, but then they began to rain down. The boys squealed and giggled as they raced madly around chasing apples. They tucked their shirts inside of their pants and loaded apples through their collars, their shirts burgeoning until the boys were round and bumpy like raspberries. Only enough apples had fallen to fill up their clothing with no room to spare. As though it suddenly dawned on them, the two boys looked around. Several yards away a woman shined an apple on the sleeve of her black dress as she smiled at them. Biting into the fruit, she disappeared around a nearby house.

Willie and Tony looked at each other for a long moment before breaking out in huge grins and tramping off to see if their mothers would bake pies for them.

David Carson glared at his wife from across the room. He had been watching her since she had reappeared from her little jaunt, the nature of which she chose not to disclose to him. He leaned across his typewriter and picked up his half-filled rock glass, tilted back his head, and threw the Scotch down his throat. He was married to a witch. Many men called their wives that, but David's wife really was. Sarinda was pale, blond and thin. Not at all like Tamara. Dark, luscious Tamara. His thoughts were always filled with her. He longed to take her, to show her a man's lovemaking; instead she gave herself to that boy.

Sarinda looked up from her sewing. It was a pastime she really enjoyed. It felt good to use her fingers. She knew he was thinking of Tamara again. He used to hide it, but of late, he didn't seem to care if she knew. She couldn't blame him. Tamara was very special, even among witches. Sarinda just didn't have that kind of fire or power. She sighed and went back to her needle. She knew David had married her only to become a witch. Mortals had such outrageous ideas about what becoming a witch really meant. They didn't realize that a true witch had to be born. It had to be in the blood. Human witches had only chants, ceremonies and trinkets to work their limited magic. Marrying a true witch only allowed them to view a ceremony, not participate in it. And the biggest ceremony of all was this coming weekend, Witches' Eve.

David rose to refill his glass. He walked around the bar, grabbing the bottle as he went. He had some research to do at the library in Butler; he reminded himself to only make it half a glass or he wouldn't be able to read a thing. He was bitter about his position among the witches. He had expected all the powers of a witch, to be privy to their secrets. Instead he now had a token membership to a select club. He had wanted Tamara, but she hadn't paid him the slightest attention. He had thought that by becoming a witch he could win Tamara over. He was strong, he was manly, he was what Tamara needed. He would have been a strong witch. Instead, now he was a namesake witch, married to another paper witch who rarely used her powers for anything. What a travesty! He who desired the powers his wife possessed and had none, and she who had them, found them distasteful. He emptied his glass again and went to the desk, selecting a notebook and pen from its drawer. He headed for the door.

"When will you be back?" Her pale eyes followed him.

"When I'm ready," he replied with the slamming of the door.

Sarinda sighed deeply. She loved him so much. She was sure now that he didn't feel the same for her. She had not chosen wisely. But how could she? His sparkling blue eyes, charming manner and smooth ways were too much for an inexperienced witch like Sarinda, despite the fact she was over two hundred years old. She had been desperately lonely and David's attention and lovemaking were a balm to Sarinda's soul. Together, their blond features would result in beautiful children, and Sarinda had always wanted to be a mother. David, though, had other ideas. It was bad enough that she had married a mortal, but to have done such a lousy job of it made her feel foolish and sad. Why hadn't she listened to the others? Perhaps she could speak with the council about selecting a new husband. She would have to wait until Witches' Eve. Only on the eve of their holiest day could she dare make such a request. Once made, the request could not be withdrawn. She had to be sure about her decision.

● ● ●

The woman came out of the house carrying a flashlight as she made her way to the barn.

"Jack?" she called, spying him at the top of a ladder that was leaning against the building. "Jack, will you come on in the house and have your supper!"

"In a minute." He continued to chip away at the paint with a scraper, his only light from a lantern.

"That's what you said an hour ago. Now come on!"

"I'm coming," he sighed, giving in. As he stepped down to the next rung, he lost his balance and fell.

"Jack!" his wife screamed.

Inches from the ground his fall halted, his body was slowly righted, and he was gently placed on his feet. The woman rushed to her husband, throwing her arms around him in relief. They both looked around, searching.

A woman in a black dress stepped from the shadows near their house. Her eyes shimmered in the night as she slowly nodded her head once. The man and woman returned the gesture and the witch moved off.

"Jack, if she hadn't been there!"

"Shhhh, it's okay. I'm alright." He kissed her on the temple as he hugged her tightly. "Can you ever remember a time when they haven't been there?" His wife shook her head and smiled shyly. "Well there ya go." His arm around his wife, they quietly returned to the house.

2

LARRY CAYLIN CLOSED his chemistry book and looked at the clock. He had four hours until the library closed and enough work to keep him busy, but his mind wouldn't let him study. Jesse Trent and what happened in the locker room filled his thoughts. He had been called on the carpet for attacking Jesse at the game. Fools, he thought to himself. If only everyone had stood against Jesse and Brentwood instead of him. But then, not everyone knew about Jesse and the witch, or at least, they didn't admit it publicly. What was the use? Tomorrow he was supposed to return to Butler College, but he didn't want to go back. He'd lost his appetite for everything and it was all Jesse's fault. Somehow, some way, Jesse Trent had to be stopped, and Larry Caylin was going to be the one to do it!

The librarian looked up from behind the book counter and blushed when she saw David Carson swing the door wide as he entered.

"Good evening, Mr. Carson," she said brightly, as she tried to control her expression toward him.

"Hello, my lovely." David flashed his winning smile. "How's tricks?" He leaned lazily on the counter, playing with her pencils and paper clips.

"Those books you ordered came in, Mr. Carson. I have them right here. I'll get them." She nervously smoothed down her skirt and tried to concentrate on finding the order. David watched her with a lecherous grin. He knew he was making her nervous. She was quite a morsel. Honey-blond hair, big blue eyes, and a shape that knocked your socks off. She blushed easily, and he often made sport of turning her three shades of crimson. She was one piece of fruit he was glad he had picked.

"Here it is." She laid the books in front of him. The bundle was tightly wrapped with brown paper and string.

"What do you say we get together tonight at your place," said David as he plucked a few tendrils of hair free from the barrette at her crown. She reddened and smoothed back her hair.

"David, please," she whispered, "we're in public. I don't want the whole town to find out!" She quickly glanced around. "Yes, that's fine with me." She blushed again.

"See you at closing, beautiful." He smiled and lightly pinched her chin. She pulled away and glanced around fearfully. David laughed to himself. She was such a silly thing. She was cute, but he knew it wouldn't be long before he moved on to other game. The world was full of women and there hadn't been one that David couldn't literally charm the pants off of. Except for Tamara.

David picked up his books and headed to the back of the library for privacy. Opening the package with a pocket knife, he found *Witches' Dialects, Spells and Incantations,* and *Devil's Sabbath,* all written by Phillip Jesoppe. Selecting the third book, David opened it and began reading.

"Okay, Mr. Jesoppe, you claim to know so much about witchcraft, tell me what I need to know!"

Tamara appeared in the kitchen as Hatisha was cooking supper. The aroma of the roasted beef filled the air as the gravy bubbled merrily. Tamara kissed Hatisha on the cheek and put her arm around her shoulders. The old witch smiled and patted the hand that rested near her neck.

"I swear, if you'd been born a mortal it wouldn't change you much!" laughed Tamara.

"Hush, child! Or you'll find yourself munching grass and shooing flies with your tail—compare me with a mortal! Ha!" teased Hatisha with a grin.

"Oh, Mother! What would you do without me? Why thee would be but an old woman with no one to listen to her complain!"

"Without thee, I'd have a clear field with that handsome young thing you're going to initiate this weekend!"

"Now how did you—," Tamara began as the two witches exchanged knowing smiles. Tamara moved to the table to sit down.

"Why, you nosy old bat, what else do you know?"

"Never a bat!" Hatisha waved a wooden spoon in the air. "A wolf, an eagle—maybe an owl or two—but never a bat!"

"Okay, okay! So you know that I plan to take him this weekend; what else do you know?"

"I know him to be a Maulkian."

Tamara leaned back against her chair, watching Hatisha check the bread that was baking in the oven. Her mother loved her cooking—a mortal occupation. All the witches except for Tamara and Essadora blatantly indulged in mortal habits. Tamara supposed it was due to all the exposure. But it was times like this that Tamara was reminded of just whom she was dealing with.

"Oh great one," she began softly, "forgive me. In my own conceit I forget that thou art my supreme."

Hatisha set down the spoon she was using and approached Tamara. Her wrinkled hands cupped the smooth, soft face. She watched as the dark eyes, filled with love and respect, looked up into her own.

"My child," Hatisha began, "you are my better. You are the product of two noble, powerful Maulkians. Your father, my son, was superior. His powers were renowned, even among our people. Your blood is untainted by mortal weakness. I'm not even sure you know the extent of your powers."

Tamara reached for the hands that held her face and took them between her own. "I know of my powers." She rose from her chair and urged Hatisha into another. Walking to the kitchen window, she began to explain:

"You know I have always believed in our race and in what our people once were. I believe that one day we shall be as numerous as the mortals are now. That we will, once again, be a great race. And to do this, we must be strong of blood, strong of principle, and strong in our powers. We must know ourselves and what we are capable of. For centuries I have felt the inner stirrings of my powers. So I have often gone out by myself to practice, alone, so I wouldn't hurt anyone had I made any mistakes. As a result, I can command life and death." Her mood was very sober.

"I don't understand," began Hatisha with concern. "What do you mean, command life and death?"

"I have found that I can create life inside the wombs of some of the lower animals."

Hatisha rose from the chair and began slowly pacing the kitchen floor, rubbing her chin with a crooked finger. "This is something, indeed. Not even the Elders could perform such a feat. Have the pregnancies come to term?"

"Just one. But the offspring was paranormal. I had to destroy it. After all, we couldn't have rabbits flying through the skies or overturning trucks on the highways, could we?"

Hatisha went to the table and sat down heavily. Tamara returned and sat beside her. Reaching out, she touched Hatisha's arm.

"Please don't worry. I will not abuse my powers." She smiled encouragingly. "You need not worry."

"Oh, my lovely, I am not worried about you. Of all the witches I've known in my lifetime, you are indeed blessed. Blessed with powers, beauty and most importantly—wisdom! It is true that you have a temper, but your capacity for justice and truth outshines all else. I am so pleased to have been a part of your creation."

"I too, am pleased. And I thank you for challenging my father."

"I didn't want to kill him." The old witch's face became grave. "He knew you were going to be very powerful." She took Tamara's hand and squeezed it tightly. "He would have destroyed you; he was very jealous. The battle was a furious one. I almost lost."

"Yes, I viewed the fight, watching from the inner universe."

"How?" Hatisha was stunned.

"I have been experimenting with time-travel. I found that if I entered the inner universe, spoke specific chants, and willed myself back to a place, I can travel through time. It is very difficult and demanding on the spirit, but I will perfect it yet." Hatisha remembered her bread and hurried to her oven as

Tamara began setting the table. Suddenly, the old witch stopped and turned back to Tamara.

"If you could move through time in any direction you chose, especially back to the past—," Hatisha began excitedly.

"I could save our race," finished Tamara. They exchanged a long look before each returned to her chores.

Tamara opened the homemade wine as her thoughts turned to the two men. "What of the two strangers? It has been some time since we have had visitors."

"One is a stranger to me. The other lived here many years ago. Now he has returned." Hatisha brought supper to the table.

"I did not sense he was of Brentwood," frowned Tamara.

"He was but a child when he left." Hatisha passed the bread to Tamara to start the meal. Her smile reminded Tamara once again whom she was dealing with.

"Why do you think he has come?"

"That is something you are better able to find out than I, daughter."

David Carson's eyes raced along the page, unable to believe what he was reading. Jesoppe went on in detail, page after page, about an ancient ceremony used by witches. The author explained that during his research he had constantly run across the symbols shown on the opposite page to the one David was reading. After all his studies, he had yet to decipher them, but he believed they were a formula for raising the Devil. David flipped quickly through the rest of the book as his heart galloped in his chest.

The symbols may have seemed foreign to Jesoppe, but they were far from that to David. One of the privileges of being a mortal witch was the introduction to the Maulkian alphabet. Made up from symbols instead of letters, it governed every communication, drawing or painting he had ever seen since his initiation. Those same three symbols illustrated in Jesoppe's book were on the cover of a leather-bound book he had seen in Hatisha's house.

He closed the book, lost in his thoughts. Jesoppe was a fool. He was so close to the truth and yet so far from it. Those symbols were that of Shining Rain, Dual Sacrifice, and of the

Receiver. Shining Rain was the power bestowed. Dual Sacrifice was always the offering to the Black Side for services rendered, and the Receiver was the one offering the sacrifice to receive the power. The ceremony was not to raise the Devil, but how to become the Devil!

David stacked the books on top of one another. As he prepared to leave, he noticed Larry Caylin sitting across the room staring into a chemistry book. Though they had never met, Larry's reputation preceded him. It was well-known throughout Brentwood and Hoopersville that Larry hated Jesse Trent's guts. Perhaps that could be used to advantage, David mused. He rose and crossed the room and sat at Larry's table, the young man looking up as he did.

"May I speak to you for a few minutes?"

"I'm busy, I don't loan money, and I already gave at the office, so beat it!" Larry stared him down. David threw back his head and laughed loudly, causing several people to tell him to be quiet. David pulled a cigarette pack from his shirt pocket and fished inside for a cigarette. He lit up with a silver lighter. Gathering his books, he rose and looked down at Larry.

"It's about a mutual foe of ours, Jesse Trent. I'm for getting rid of the bastard. If you're interested, I'll be in the parking lot." He strode quickly away. Passing the librarian, he patted her bottom. "Not tonight, dear, I've got a headache!" He laughed again as he pushed out the library door.

The night was warm but the air smelled of rain. He looked up at the stars twinkling above him before he let his gaze wander in the direction of Brentwood. A circle of purple bloated clouds hovered in the gray-blue sky above the town, threatening to unleash their burden long before his return. Some would say the sight of clouds only above Brentwood was a trick of the light, but David knew it was concocted by the witches just for the occasion. The witches liked the warm weather with rain at night during this time of year. If he hadn't seen their magic for himself, he would have never believed it existed.

"So?" Larry watched David with a careful look. David leaned against his car and smoked his cigarette with a relaxed calm that irked Larry. His arms were folded across his chest as he stared at the sky over Brentwood.

"Stop wasting time and tell me—," began Larry.

"You've got to learn to become more patient. Otherwise, you'll wind up a nervous old man," smiled David as he dropped the cigarette butt to the ground and crushed it out. "Do you believe in witches?" he asked seriously.

"There's no such thing as—"

"Then why do you hate Jesse Trent so much?" David studied Larry as he shifted his books to his other arm.

"You said that you hated Jesse too. I suppose that means that *you* believe in witches?"

"Let's just say that Jesse Trent has been a thorn in my side for quite some time. I want the woman he has."

"You mean the witch?" Larry joined David by sitting on the hood of the car.

"I thought you said you didn't believe in witches?"

"Well, nobody else does. At least they don't admit it." His look became far away as he leaned forward and rested his arms on his knees. "But things have been different since I went away to college. . . . It's like a veil was lifted from my brain. We all just accepted it in Brentwood 'cause we grew up with it. But I can't accept it anymore." His look hardened and he gave David his full attention. "Now, what have you got on your mind?"

"What I've got on my mind is getting rid of Jesse Trent and winning over Tamara to me. You can be in charge of Trent's destruction and I'll take care of *her*. . . ."

"I'm going to get caught in the rain," Tamara said to her mother.

"A little water never hurt anyone—except, of course, you were a mortal at the witch hunts where they tied their victims up and threw them into the river. If they floated, they were witches, if not—well, then it didn't much matter." Hatisha finished clearing the dishes.

"If I'm going, I'd better hurry. I want to be back before the rain, and before our meeting starts." Tamara opened her arms above her head in an arc. Her dress disappeared, leaving her naked as it reappeared over the back of the dining chair. She was a beauty. Though she had never carried a child, she had the body of a matured woman. Her legs were strong and sleek, her back lean and supple, with curving hips, flat belly and proud, full breasts. She looked to be in her midtwenties, but she was actually several centuries old. Witches never cared much for mortal time. Hatisha sighed at the sight of her.

"If I hadn't fought your father, I'd still look like you." Hatisha stroked her daughter's dark, thick hair that cascaded down to the middle of her back, and she arranged it around Tamara's shoulders.

"I have fought others in the past and it has not affected me so, why then thee?" she asked, startled.

"Ah, daughter. You see, one must not try and change the enemy, but destroy him. I didn't want to kill your father. I wanted to reduce his powers or take them away so that he would not harm you. In the end, he died and I lost my power to retain my youth; I was lucky I wasn't killed too." The old witch gave her a hug. "It is time, how will you go?" she asked as Tamara moved to the center of the kitchen.

"I guess I'll go as a cat." She shrugged. Hatisha roared with laughter. "Well, I haven't got time to think up anything else!" added Tamara, perturbed.

"Yes, but that's a bit theatrical, don't you think? I mean, after all, every mortal on this planet is convinced that cats and witches are one and the same! They call them familiars."

"Yes, Mother! Now can I get on with it?"

"Excuse the snickering of an old woman, please be my guest. But I ask just one favor."

"What?"

"Any color but black!" Hatisha put her finger against her mouth to keep from laughing.

Tamara stretched her arms above her head and formed a triangle with her fingers. With her elbows slightly bent and the triangle directly over her head, she closed her eyes and began to move her lips in silent chant. She started to glow a bright green, and then the color of pure light. She moved the triangle until it was in front of her, opened her eyes, and looked up into the triangle. Two rays of blinding brilliance shot out of her eyes and into the triangle with a thundering sound. Then she began to transform before Hatisha.

Her back arched, her legs hunched and a tail began to grow from her spine. Her hands balled as the fingers receded into the palms. The nails became claws. Soft, brown fur began to grow on the naked animal that stood in the center of the light. Tamara was gone. In her place, as the thunder died out, stood a shiny, brown cat the size of a panther. Hatisha clapped her hands and squealed with the delight of a child.

"Oh, but I do admire the work of a true artist!" The cat looked at her and transmitted its thoughts. *If you don't mind, a little help if you please.* The cat's tail swished irritably.

"With pleasure," said Hatisha as she made an eloquent, sweeping bow. She began chanting silently as she moved her hands in a circle above the huge cat. As she finished her movements, the cat began to shrink down. Hatisha opened the kitchen window and turned back to the cat, which had shrunk to the size of a house cat.

"Let me help you, my dear." She picked up the cat and scratched its ears. "You make a beautiful cat as well." Then, Hatisha unceremoniously tossed the cat out of the first floor window, calling after it, "Don't get wet, dearie!" She slammed the window with a rattle of the glass, and laughed again.

The cat ran through the night streets as above her the brooding sky, filled with churning clouds, carried on a spectacular slow-motion ballet. The cat paid no attention, having seen the eerie sight more times than she cared to remember. Once put into motion by the Maulkians for the Eve, it would not be stopped, for it served a purpose. It reminded the mortals of how awesome the witches could be, so that no fools would venture out on the Eve.

Even from this distance, she could feel her mother's laughter. She didn't resent it, she was glad for it. The two of them had shared many things over the centuries and she prayed for several more together. Laughter was a sign that all was well.

She slowed as she circled the boarding house, using Maulkian senses to find which room the two men had taken. Much to her pleasure, she discovered they had taken a room off of the fire escape. Crouching under the wooden ladder which rested off the ground, she marshaled all of her strength. With speed and deftness, the cat leapt to the platform. She bounded up the stairs to the correct window and looked in. The curtains were open, and Paul, as she had heard the other call him, was lying on the bed, watching television, wearing only boxer shorts. At least if they had nothing interesting to say, they would be pleasing to look at.

Richard emerged from the bathroom. Fresh from his shower, he was clad in nothing as he dried himself with a towel. She moved closer to the window for a better look.

"First thing tomorrow, I'll give you a tour of Brentwood. I'll show you a house that's supposed to belong to a witch. At least it did when I was living here." Richard dried his hair. "What are you watching, anyway?"

"Abbott and Costello Meet Godzilla," replied Paul without looking up.

"Your momma!" Richard threw the towel at him and returned to the bathroom. Paul grinned as he blocked the shot and continued watching television.

The cat moved to a different angle to get a view into the bathroom. Richard looked like she imagined Jesse would look when he matured physically. The ten years that separated Jesse and Richard made quite a difference. The cat purred at the thought of Jesse maturing into that kind of man. . . .

The pebble ricocheted within the sill of the second-story window, finally coming to a rest in a small, dense spider web. At first, fear kept the small spider crouched tightly in the sill's corner, but then, when the intruder no longer moved, the indignant, eight-legged creature moved off to find a new home.

The window noiselessly slid up and open, and Bobby stuck his head out searchingly. Larry signaled him to come down, and then silently disappeared back into the trees. In jeans and bare feet, pulling on his shirt, Bobby deftly traversed the roof toward the old, tired tree leaning dramatically beside the house. With seasoned grace, Bobby leapt into the air, grabbing the ancient branch like a trapeze bar, his weight gently forcing it to the ground. He grinned as his stomach tightened with the free flight and a feeling he hoped never to get over. Life was so much easier when you were a child, so simple. The branch snapped back into place without any damage to itself, for this was a ritual performed countlessly over the last eighteen years. As he headed into the trees, heaviness again overtook him.

Yes, childhood was simple, but he was an adult now and it was time to face the demon his friend wrestled with. He knew what tone the conversation would take because it wasn't that late; Larry could have come to the front door if he wanted to talk to Bobby, but he hadn't.

Bobby picked his way through the twigs until he stood by his friend. "What's up?"

"I'm gonna get Jesse."

"What are you talkin' about?" A sigh escaped his lips.

"I met this guy at the library tonight. He's found a way to take care of Jesse." Larry's face was tired, but his eyes shone in the darkness.

"What do you mean, take care of Jesse?"

Larry turned away and picked at the bark of the nearest tree. "Jesse's not like us. There's somethin' *wrong* about him. Somethin' evil. And my daddy says when somethin' evil threatens you . . . you kill it."

"Damn it, Larry!" Bobby blurted out. He pressed against the trunk of the tree that Larry still picked at, his arm wrapped around the trunk, almost as a support.

"I thought you hated him too?"

"Sure, but you can't kill a human being!"

"He ain't human," Larry said emotionlessly.

"He is! He eats, sleeps, and bleeds! Don't you remember the time in football when he cut his knee on the field? That was real! So he plays like God, so what? He's real! He's human!" His voice broke. "Don't do this to yourself."

"You're on his side."

"You're so stupid." Bobby half laughed. Shaking his head, he turned away and stared out across the dark fields. "I'm the best friend you've ever had. You're my brother, you know that. Please, whatever this guy is gonna do, don't get involved."

Larry pressed his hand over his eyes and sighed. "Yeah, you're right. Sorry." He moved beside Bobby and looked out over the fields. "It's all the excitement of bein' home. Goin' back to school tomorrow. You're lucky you ain't goin' tomorrow, what a hassle!"

"I wish I was," smiled Bobby. "You don't know how boring it is not havin' you around. All I do anymore is work."

Bobby studied his friend carefully. Larry smiled and put his hand on Bobby's shoulder.

"Don't worry about me. I'm okay." He moved away, the intimacy scaring him off to a safer distance. "I guess I was just tired. Too much happening. I gotta go."

"What about Jesse?"

"Ah, screw Jesse. He'll probably marry the prettiest girl in the county, have seven kids and she'll get fat, grow a beard and wear the britches in the family!" They both laughed at his joke and the tension seemed to break.

"Write me from school, okay? We should talk more."

"I will." Larry moved through the trees, and then stopped suddenly. Turning back to Bobby, his face filled with emotion, he said, "Good-bye, Bobby." Then he strode away.

"See ya!" Bobby called to his friend's disappearing back, wondering why the words sounded so final.

3

An almost inaudible sound reached the cat's ears. She turned quickly to her left, rising to all fours. A multicolored alley cat stood staring at her with intense interest. A soft growl emitted from the male's throat as he approached her. She hunched her back into the grandest arch she could muster and screamed at him. It only served to heighten his excitement. He rolled to his back before her and playfully took a swipe at her. She was very annoyed that such a creature should happen along at this very moment.

Tamara slapped him, claws bared. The male leapt to its feet and crouched in a wary position. A typical male, Tamara thought, he just wouldn't take no for an answer. She was possessed of greater thought, agility and strength than the cat before her, but if she was to beat him, she had to do it as a cat. The alternatives were to either transform in front of the men, or to abandon her surveillance and come back later.

The two animals circled one another, their eyes blazing in the night. The male leapt on her, trying to maneuver behind. She rolled to her back, claws flying wildly, bent on drawing blood.

Richard pulled up his cotton pajama bottoms and moved into the room. It was so hot, he wasn't sure he even wanted to sleep in them in the first place, but one thing he had learned traveling on assignment, you always had to be ready for anything. Suddenly, a wild scream penetrated the room, causing Richard to freeze in his tracks and Paul to jump from the bed.

"What the hell was that?" whispered Paul. The scream came again, drawing both Paul and Richard to the window.

"Look! Cats, and are they goin' at it!" said Paul almost gleefully. Richard opened the window and the feline came flying in, grateful for the escape. The male had had enough. He tore down the fire escape, glad to be rid of her. He had had love on his mind, not war; he knew where to find more willing females.

She slipped quickly under the first bed. Silently, she hurried among the equipment hidden in the darkness. Her eyes began to glow as she viewed each box intently. The glow disappeared as the cat emerged from under the bed.

Richard watched the cat jump on his bed and make herself at home. He moved to the bed and crawled over to her and laid down on his side. He began stroking the soft, brown fur. The cat rubbed against him, purring softly, like a running motor.

"It's not hard to guess what sort of male she's interested in," Paul said, smirking as he shut the window and crossed to the air conditioning vent on the far wall. "I'd say the old boy never stood a chance!" He banged on the vent. "I'm not havin' the best o' luck with air conditioners lately." He returned to his own bed and focused his attention on the TV set.

Picking up the cat, Richard rolled to his back, placing her on his chest. Her eyes engaged his in a long moment. She was a beautiful animal. He scratched her ears and stroked back the fur on her face, checking for injury. There was none. Paul noticed Richard's preoccupation.

"That's the most attention you've paid to a female since Debra." The cat's ears seemed to perk up at his remark as Paul moved to the end of Richard's bed.

"I don't want to talk about it," Richard said quietly as he continued to pet the silky fur.

"You've been living like a goddamned hermit. Nothing but work for the last seven months. I'm tellin' you, you're getting pretty dull. I bet that's why Nate decided to let you do this story. It's the first thing you've been interested in for a long while."

"Give it a rest, okay?" Richard sat up and set the cat in his lap. She curled up on her side and laid her head on Richard's leg near his knee. She stretched out the paw that lay against his leg, which allowed her to roll more to her back and watch his face.

"So what else are we going to do besides look at houses that are supposed to belong to witches?" Paul asked, relenting and changing the subject.

"I'll give you a tour of Brentwood. Then we'll go to the library—it's not very big, most of the informative stuff will be in the library in Butler. But the local documents will be here and I'll show you that, barring accidents, the people in Brentwood only die of old age. There's no doctor."

"No doctor?" Paul said. "What do they do for medical care?"

"I told you, witches." Richard thought the cat had stopped purring, but he still felt the motor under his touch.

"So if someone gets sick, they go to this witch and get cured, is that what you're saying?"

Outside, the clouds burst under their burden and the warm rain fell to the earth. The cat let out a low meow, seemingly bothered by the sound of the rain tapping lightly on the window glass. Richard stroked the cat again, calming her.

"Let's call it a night, I want to get an early start tomorrow." Richard rose from the bed, causing the cat to tumble out of his lap. As he set the alarm on his watch for six-thirty, the cat's eyes followed his every movement. Paul pushed the off button on the color set and dove into his own bed. As Richard pulled back his covers, the cat walked to his pillow and made herself comfortable.

"Don't you wish all women were that easy to lure to your bed?" Paul said, grinning from across the room. Richard picked up the cat and held her gently in his arms. Scratching her head as he nuzzled her with his face, he approached the window.

"You'd better get home, little girl. A cat as pretty as you must live somewhere nearby. If you were mine, I wouldn't want you out at all hours." Richard opened the window and set the cat out on the fire escape. The window shut with a bang before the cat came to fully appreciate her situation. She was getting soaked by the downpour. Quickly, she crept down the slick stairway and leapt to the ground. She began to run as fast as her legs could carry her.

The cat went on through the night, traversing alleyways and back lots. Gracefully, her legs stretched outward, her claws digging into the earth, grabbing for speed. She grew, her size increasing with every stride. Soon the panther encountered a six-foot fence in her path. Without breaking stride, the panther headed for it. The huge cat leapt into the air, clearing the fence with graceful agility. Her landing was flawless despite the rain, and she continued her journey. Soon, she rose on two legs as the hair and claws receded. The hunched legs smoothed out to long, firm thighs. She slowed her pace, coming to a stop amid the shadows.

As she materialized in the kitchen, the first thing Tamara saw was Hatisha standing in front of her.

"I knew thee would get caught in the rain," Hatisha said in greeting as she wrapped Tamara with sparkling magic that became a huge, soft towel.

"Blessed be, my mother." Tamara seated herself at the table, pulling the towel tighter. The water dripping down her body into the towel suited her somber mood. She had no desire to hurry into her robes. The old woman put an empty mug in front of her daughter. Waving her wrinkled hand over it, she began stirring the empty cup with her forefinger, and piping hot tea rose to fill the cup as steam spiraled upward.

"You're welcome, my dear. How was your journey?" Hatisha sat herself down to listen.

"Interesting." Tamara sipped at the bubbling concoction. Hot tea after a warm rain was to the Maulkians what liquor on a cold day was to the mortals. "They have come here for the ceremony. They wish to observe, or rather, to expose our traditions." Tamara looked thoughtfully into the cup, watching the steam dance across the liquid surface. "Why must mortals be so curious?" Her features grew dark with worry. "It will be a shame to have to kill them."

"Why so severe?" Hatisha looked at her daughter with interest. She knew Tamara was merely thinking out loud.

Tamara rose and dried herself with magic as the towel

disappeared and her robes gently glided into place. "These two are dangerous. They are reporters. We can't simply wipe their memories and send them home. That would only fuel their theories that we are far from mortals practicing witchcraft. No, these two will have to be dealt with in total seriousness and with great care. They have brought special equipment with them. Cameras and recording devices are hidden under their beds; I took a good look at them before I settled in for my eavesdropping."

"Did they say that they expected the rituals of the mortal witches, or have we finally been discovered?"

"That's the puzzling part. When they first arrived, the one called Richard spoke of us as mortal occultists."

"Richard would be the one who lived among us years ago?"

"Yes, that's right. He called us hysterical crazies, scaring the town into paying homage to us. But this evening in their room, he knew that no one in Brentwood dies prematurely. He knew also that Brentwood has no doctor."

"Your point?" Hatisha leaned forward.

"In his heart, he believes. A believer will be harder to fool than a skeptic." Tamara began pacing the room irritably. The old woman watched her with experienced eyes.

"If you are going to talk to me, you must do it now, before the others arrive."

Tamara looked out the window to the misting rain. The downpour had stopped, leaving the warm, wet mist hanging in the air. The temperature hadn't dipped below the eighties, despite the wet.

"Why did he have to come here now?" She ran her long nails through her hair and then pulled it to the top of her head.

"You are moved by him?" asked Hatisha as she raised an imperious finger at the cupboard and levitated three bottles of her homemade wine to the center of the table, along with several glasses.

"Yes, very. I am torn, torn." She let her hair fall around her shoulders and returned to the table to sit.

"What causes the indecision?" Hatisha poured wine for the two of them. "If you want him, then take him."

"I can't! How can I deny to Jesse what I allow for myself?"

"You may do as you please. You are a Maulkian."

"And so is Jesse!"

"Not until after the Eve. Before that time he is but a mortal, vying for your attention." Hatisha sipped her wine.

"I plan to join with Jesse. We have pledged to spend our lives together." Tamara swallowed half of the wine in her glass before she studied the goblet broodingly.

"You ask for heartache," sighed Hatisha. "It has been some time since two Maulkians have pledged to one another. What will you do when another witch wants to mate with Jesse and you cannot deny her?" Hatisha refilled Tamara's glass.

"No other witch would dare to ask to mate with him."

"You forget Essadora."

"I will handle Essadora."

"She is strong. And you are not her favorite. She may take Jesse just to spite you."

"Let her try!" She bolted up from her chair and circled the room like a bull waiting to be released into the arena. Hatisha leaned back to watch the fire burning in her daughter's eyes. "You cannot deny her."

"I will!" Tamara slammed her hands on the table in front of her mother. She leaned close to Hatisha.

"I have perfected the Ab En Caam!"

"No!" Hatisha uttered breathlessly. Chills ran through her. "Not since the Elders—"

"Until now! I can intensify the special chemicals in Jesse's blood to make him a full-blooded Maulkian Witch. I went back in time to the scene of my father's defeat and gathered the hair from my own father's head as he lay dying after your battle. I crushed it in a mortar with a pestle made from the bone of my last rib. I mixed the hair with Heeca and Taferand, added blood from my cycle and boiled all to make the ointment that I rub nightly into Jesse's skin. Every time we make love, I chant the Ab En Caam. On Witches' Eve, I and I alone will lie with Jesse. But instead of a mere mortal initiated into the coven, Jesse will become the first Maulkian Witch to be created before your eyes!" Her intensity seemed to startle even her. She paused, collected herself, and then straightening up, she continued in her usual, calm manner. "He will transform before your very eyes. I vowed never to mate outside of my race and I will keep my promise. Jesse will be all that I am because he comes from my history as well as his own. His grandparents were witches and so shall he be again.'' She returned to her seat. ''I must be the one to take him on Witches' Eve. If someone else takes him, the results could be disasterous. Only I know the secret. Only I know the correct chants. If Jesse is exposed to his powers prematurely, he could kill us all.''

Sarinda materialized in Hatisha's kitchen right on time. She was always punctual; being late was not the way to stay in Hatisha's good graces. But on this particular occasion, she had the feeling that she should have arrived at least two minutes late, for the look held tightly by Tamara and Hatisha wasn't meant for intrusion. But before she could say or do anything, Hatisha smiled amicably and motioned for her to sit at the large, round kitchen table. As soon as she was seated, the others began arriving.

Braneesa, Corcha, and Mazinna arrived together in a collage of glittering, colored radiance, chattering nonstop. All wore black robes rimmed in the color chosen by the Maulkian to express her inner spirit. Their attire consisted of two robes: The black outer robe and an inner robe of shimmering color. The centers of the robes were cut to form a collar, with a slit opening that plunged down the front to the waist. There were no buttons or zippers at this opening, the material simply held itself shut like a seam that could be opened easily, but only by the touch of a witch. Both robes were kidney-shaped so that sleeves were formed within the yards of material by raising one's arms out to the sides. The inner robe was larger than the outer, thereby forming a one-inch border of color completely around the rim of the black outer robe. Despite the mass of material in the robes, their weight was no more than tissue paper.

Braneesa was an aristocratic-looking Maulkian with long, blond hair that spilled across her shoulders and down to the middle of her back. Her robes were rimmed in rich brown and she wore no color on her long nails, preferring their natural beauty. Her pointed nose and high cheekbones helped lend the air of royalty about her. Her behavior was unreproachable; she could always be counted on to do the right thing.

After Hatisha, Braneesa was the oldest Maulkian in Brentwood. She was born in Macedonia during the reign of Philip II and spent the next centuries of her life migrating to various cities all across Europe. She would see the rise and fall of the Roman Empire. The births and deaths of kings. Until finally, separated from her parents during the witch hunts of the eighteenth century, she was forced to sail for the new world, a place later called America.

Corcha's green-rimmed robes highlighted her blue-green eyes; her lips were full and moist, accentuating the sexually alluring face. Though all the Maulkians but Hatisha were beautiful by mortal standards, each had her own stamp and Corcha clearly knew hers.

Born in Mesopotamia, she made her way across the Roman Empire as a kept woman of high-born men and military leaders until she became a victim of one of the groups of religious fanatics who called themselves Christians. Afterward, wary of mortals, Corcha wandered the continent in search of her own kind, a search that would take her to distant shores.

Along with Braneesa and Corcha, Mazinna took her seat at the table and arranged her yellow-rimmed robes about her. She had been reared in the English countryside and in the court of Henry VIII.

Washka and Fleena, the inseparable pair, sat across from Mazinna. Born to different mothers in the American Midwest, they shared the same father. And last—alone—Essadora arrived, taking her appointed seat as she acknowledged everyone's presence, carefully avoiding Tamara. It was better for all if they ignored one another. Her inner color was gold, which seemed at odds with the lavender color she wore on her long, razor-sharp nails. Her dark brunette hair was accented by two wide stripes of silver color that started at each of her temples and followed the line of her hair away from her face and down to the middle of her back.

Nine witches completed the circle. Nine women, the last remnants of a dying breed. All, save for Hatisha, were young and beautiful. Each bore a name ending with an "A" to denote the Maulkian symbol for power. The chain completed, they raised their glasses as was their custom, and Hatisha chanted their blessing. Like all their chants it was silent, to keep outsiders and unbelievers from knowing the words.

Hatisha wore her robes of black and purple with the pride of a Maulkian, but she was lost in reverie. She was remembering the birth of her son Menchant, in the place now called Transylvania. It was a time of controversy and upheaval for the witches. They were spreading to the four corners of the globe, losing their traditions, destroying or being destroyed by the mortals out of fear and ignorance. A great leader was needed among the witches to pull them back together as the Great Tachmann had once done. But it was becoming increasingly difficult to find a place that was not tainted by mortals, and in their quest for solitude the witches had broken away from their roots.

Hatisha was determined to pull her race together again. She had hoped her son would grow to be the leader needed to rally her people, but Menchant, like all Earthian born, was arrogant, prideful and wild with only his self-interest to guide his deeds.

Her hopes were to find a place of solitude to raise another child without mortal contamination. But the child had to be of pure blood and of good stock, fresh in the Maulkian spirit. Though the witches had been resorting to incest since the diminishing of their numbers, Hatisha had so far avoided inter-breeding. But now her son was the only male witch whose heritage she could be sure of.

Unfortunately, the mating ritual caused a change in Menchant. Instead of going off at the end of the ceremony as was usual with the males of her race, he stayed. Hatisha made her plans for departure as she waited for the birth of her child and grandchild. At Tamara's birth Hatisha learned the reason for Menchant's continued watch over her pregnancy. As Hatisha's child, Menchant had powers few Earth-born possessed. He was a truly gifted witch, admired by all, and looked upon almost as a god—and he wanted it kept that way.

Hatisha had never cared much for ostentatious displays of magic without a purpose, so she never did anything to take the spotlight from her son, though she was just as powerful. Menchant was worried that this newborn infant might be as powerful as he, perhaps more powerful, and might win the hearts of his people.

Menchant went to Hatisha's small cottage in the hills,

determined to take Tamara from her mother. But when he entered, the baby was alone, but Hatisha had surrounded the cradle with a shield of twinkling magic. The cradle was completely encircled by this dazzling barrier that allowed air, light, and sound to travel throughout unhindered, but was completely unpenetrable by anyone else. Menchant stood above the barrier and looked down at his child and sister. She was beautiful—resembling Hatisha—and she even smiled up at her father, in recognition.

Menchant turned the palms of his hands to the barrier, sending a blast of electrical energy to assault it. As he poured more and more energy through his palms, the barrier continued to resist, glowing a brighter and brighter red as the friction increased. Suddenly there was a small explosion around the barrier and all the energy that Menchant had been pouring into it was thrown back at him, sending him flying back against the wall of the cottage. Angered, he slowly rose to his feet and stood once again before the protected cradle. He closed his fists tightly and put them to his temples. Closing his eyes, he visualized the barrier and used his thoughts to transform it into a fragile egg shell. His mind then reached around the egg and crushed it. Though the image was destroyed, the barrier remained intact. Enraged, Menchant slammed his fists against the barrier and was quickly sorry. The barrier stung him mercilessly, again sending him flying back. Menchant screamed out his rage and began calling on the forces of black magic to aid him. As with any service rendered by the black side, a payment was required, and Menchant intended to pay with Tamara's life. He formed a triangle with his hands and silently chanted as he waited for the black side to respond. The entire room grew dark and thunder filled the small cottage as bolts of electrical charges crackled through the air. Opening his arms in a wide arc over his head, his palms upwards, Menchant received the power, the electrical charges converging in his hands. His eyes glowed bright red and he found himself giddy with the feeling of strength pouring through him. He pointed one finger at the barrier surrounding the cradle and let loose the incredible force now within him, splitting the barrier in two like an over-ripe melon.

Not far away, Hatisha slipped her robes over her head and

straightened them around herself. Fresh from bathing in a secluded pond in the woods near her cottage, her beautiful figure tingled with the slight chill in the air. She twisted her hair into a long braid down the middle of her back before picking up the basket of herbs she had been out collecting. She had decided that the herbs this place offered were barely any use to her and that, if she was going to augment her powers, she was going to have to raise her own specialized garden.

Suddenly, the forces around her trembled. Someone had called on the black side for its services. She lifted her robes and walked quickly toward home, trying to sense who it was. The basket dropped from her hands as her inner eye saw Menchant receive the power in her own cottage. Instantly she evaporated into twinkling radiance as Menchant split the barrier.

Laughing, Menchant reached inside the now defunct barrier and lifted Tamara out. She cooed at him, her dark eyes lovingly examining him as he held her over the cradle to examine her. She was a beautiful baby; creamy skin, pink lips and a delicate neck that looked as though it would snap like a twig. Too bad, he thought smugly. She might have been worth the wait of her growing up, just so he could have her, at least once. But he couldn't risk it. Not even for one night of pleasure.

A crippling bolt of magic bore into his back and he dropped Tamara out of shock. She landed inside her cradle with a plop. Though unhurt, she screamed with indignation over her treatment. Staggering, Menchant wheeled around to face his mother.

"You will not kill my child."

"I must! She will be powerful, I can't let her live!"

"She's your sister! Can you kill one of your own blood?"

"I am the greatest Maulkian. I will not let her take that from me!"

"You have taken it from yourself!" Hatisha waved her fingers toward the cradle, causing Tamara to disappear.

"No! You must not take her! The black side will demand payment!"

"Then you must pay the debt yourself." Hatisha left the

cottage and moved to the small clearing in front. Recovered from her surprise attack, Menchant pursued her. Hatisha readied herself for his assault. She knew she could not go to Tamara without him following. They circled one another cautiously as they studied each other. For the first time, Menchant questioned the strength of his own power against his mother. They were of the pure blood and in the past he had only faced the others. It would indeed be a struggle. Only the best would survive.

The old crone toddered into the nearby cave and made her way deep into its bowels. Steam rose from the natural hot springs within to create eerie mist figures that would disperse and form again. The accumulating steam would collect at the top of the cave and rain down in periodic drips.

Coming to a dry section of the underground shelter, the old witch's look rested on a sleeping Tamara, nestled in a bed of straw. Hatisha settled down next to her daughter and began to weep. She had saved her child, she had killed her child. There was nothing fair about the world, or about life. Why must something always be given up in order to gain? She looked at her withered, gnarled hands and lifted them to her face, tracing the wrinkles deeply etched into her skin. Her youth and beauty would have been a reasonable price to pay to keep her son alive, but the black side had demanded more payment. She had been unable to prevent the dark side from draining the life from her son, and she could not offer herself in his place, for her own youth had begun draining from her as her body shrunk and twisted to its new form. Had Menchant not made the evil pact, he would have lived the rest of his life as a mortal. Now he would not live at all except as energy used by the black side for its evil purposes.

Tamara stirred beside her mother and began fussing for her supper. Pulling open her robes out of habit, Hatisha had picked up Tamara to feed her before she remembered; she had no milk. She was an old woman now. Her weeping intensified, but Tamara's insistence brought her back to the importance at hand. With a wave of her fingers, a goat materialized in the cave and Hatisha used her to suckle Tamara.

● ● ●

The angry mob pressed on through the forest even though the sun was setting fast and any normal, god-fearing person would not be out after nightfall. They carried picks, hoes, knives, sickles—anything sharp, anything lethal—to a witch. They began lighting torches as the night settled around them. They had caught sight of her several times; she was not far away. They would not abandon the search now.

The young woman stumbled through the thick trees and bushes as the limbs and thorns scratched her skin, tore at her hair and ripped her robes. Her pregnant belly kept her from moving faster by sending crippling waves of pain throughout her body. Her baby was demanding to be born and she could deny it no longer. She collapsed onto the moss-covered floor of a forest in the heart of a place called Germany.

Witch, they had called her. She turned to her back and pulled up her robes, spreading her legs wide as another wave radiated through her belly. She knew she was gifted with a few abilities, but she had only used them to heal—never to harm, why did they pursue her? An uncontrollable urge to push brought her up and forward as she held her breath and bore down. She had noticed their coolness of late, their questioning glances. Perhaps it had been the new priest who had come to live in the village. He had visited her house to ask why she didn't attend mass with the others, while she was working to save a feverish boy who had been brought to her by his parents. He had watched her for a few minutes before crossing himself and leaving. She pushed again. The child tumbled amid the moss and leaves and lay squalling as it glistened with birth fluid. The young girl collapsed back in relief as she stared at the sky. This was her first child. It had also been the first time she had ever mated. He had been the only male of her kind she had ever known. It was a year of firsts, it seemed. The urge to push came again and she sat up gladly, knowing this was to be the placenta and the last of the birth. It was done. She rested her arms on her legs as she looked at the baby. She was a tiny, weak-looking little thing. Her eyes were pale like her father's and her color didn't look good. She would need a lot of care—care that a fleeing woman could not give her.

The sound of the mob was getting closer and panic pressed upon her once again. She had to make a decision quickly.

The men were moving so quickly that they almost stepped on the child lying on the ground. They stood in stunned silence as the little girl squirmed quietly, flexing her fingers and feet.

"I told you! I told you!" harped a short fat man. "Only a witch would abandon a baby! She's a witch, I tell ya!" The crowd agreed.

"But what do we do with the child?" asked someone from the interior of the mob.

"Kill it! Kill it!" came several replies. "It's a witch, just the same as she was! It's a demon!"

"Wait!" A tall man, more subdued than the rest, stepped forward and picked the child up. "If it be a witch, there is a way to tell."

"Throw it in the river! Witches can't stand water!"

"Yeah!" The group was in total agreement.

They approached the river, its gurgling, churning swiftness cutting a deep gorge through the mountains of the forest. The somber man held the child above him to cast the little girl in, but he couldn't bring himself to do it. The fat man held out his hands.

"I'll do it. I'm not afraid of witches!"

"I'm not afraid of witches," began the somber man as he handed over the child. "I'm just afraid that the child is not a witch."

"Her mother is a witch and so is she!" cried the other, throwing the child into the raging torrent.

Several hundred yards downstream, Hatisha and Tamara climbed along the far side of the gorge. Tamara was now a young girl. A mortal might consider her to be sixteen, but mortal years had no relation to witch time. Hatisha stopped suddenly and straightened up as much as her back would permit.

"What is it, my mother?"

"A disturbance." Hatisha's quick eyes searched the river banks.

"You mean the mortals up-river?"

"No, a witch." Tamara fell silent as she paid attention to every move her mother made. School was in session.

Hatisha scanned the entire area with her inner eye. She could sense that a witch had come through this way very recently, but she had found a horse and ridden off very swiftly. She was not an experienced witch, especially if she preferred that way of travel instead of the inner universe. But the scent of a witch still lingered, too strong for the witch to not be there.

Suddenly, it seemed as though the witch passed below them and moved away at a swift pace.

"I too have felt it." Tamara touched her mother's arm as they both looked in the direction of the witch scent. Hatisha quickly reached out with her right hand and waved it with a fluid motion before grasping the air and using a lifting motion. From downstream, the child lifted out of the water and came toward the witches on top of the gorge as Hatisha waved her hand toward herself.

The lifeless little body landed gently in Hatisha's arms. She laid it on its stomach over her arm and pressed on its back, driving water from its lungs.

"Stupid mortals!" hissed Tamara as she tore her look from the dead child. She walked a little bit away from where her mother worked carefully on the child and her inner eye traveled to the men who were now returning to their village. She lifted her hands into the air, tilted her chin to the sky, and began to chant silently.

The clouds gathered swiftly over the men and they stopped in their tracks to look above them as thunder rumbled through the clouds and a lightning bolt split the darkness behind them. The night crackled with electricity as the image of the baby appeared, floating gently a few feet off the ground, still dripping with water. The men huddled together, frozen with horror at the manifestation. The baby's eyes were closed as Tamara's voice came from its open mouth.

"You—have—sinned!" echoed the ominous voice over the low rumbling from the clouds. "You—have—murdered! You—will—be—punished!" The baby's eyes opened, but there were no pupils, only white orbs staring at the men. Suddenly, fangs appeared in the baby's mouth and claws on its fingers as the sound of a demon wailed at the terrified men. The terrible image of the baby lunged at the mob, scattering them in every direction.

"Enough of your foolishness. Come, I need you now," scolded Hatisha as she motioned Tamara over to her. She held the baby in the crook of her arm and covered it with the sleeve of her robe with the other arm.

"I am sorry, my mother. I could not help myself. I was more lenient than he deserved." Tamara covered her face with her hands as she concentrated, her hands beginning to glow with a beautiful blue light. Taking her hands from her face, she pressed them together as if in prayer as she chanted silently. Then she laid her hands on the robes that covered the infant, and the blue light intensified. When the glow subsided, Tamara's eyes began to radiate with power and a brilliant light shot from both eyes into the robes where Hatisha held the child.

Tamara's clouds had long since dispersed and only the beauty of twinkling stars filled the night sky above the women. Hatisha drew back the sleeve of her robe and the baby squealed and gurgled at her, sucking on her tiny fist. Hatisha and Tamara looked up into each other's eyes and smiled.

"What shall we call her?" Tamara's wry grin said that she knew how much her mother loved babies. Hatisha cooed at the infant and rocked her gently in her arms as she waltzed the child around the bluff above the gorge.

"She is a weak child," began Hatisha as she smiled lovingly at the baby, tickling her chin with a crooked finger, "and she will need much care. But she is a happy child. Gentle. I shall call her Sarinda."

The women moved on, Hatisha carrying Sarinda in her robes for protection. They traveled for several miles before taking refuge in a cave. The baby had begun to whimper fretfully.

"Sarinda must be fed."

Tamara looked up quickly at her mother as her meaning sank in.

"You don't mean me!"

"I'd do it myself, but my equipment's not what it once was."

"Surely you're joking?"

"Well, do you know of a cow or goat that can be brought here to feed her?"

"No, but—"

"Then there's no other way."

"I'll find one, I'll find one!" Tamara rose quickly and left the cave. Hatisha picked up Sarinda and cradled her in her arms.

"Don't worry my little one. She will find some milk, or she will feed you herself. She's just afraid of getting too attached to you. We witches seem to forever be on the losing end when we form attachments. And too, I suspect, she's a tiny bit jealous. She has always had me to herself. But fear not, if need be, she will protect you with her life—as I will. I swear it!"

Hatisha dragged herself back from memories, and began to joke and laugh with the others. They had all drunk deeply of the good wine, and were full of stories about the weakness of mortals and the legendary strength of masterful witches. It seemed that only at these gatherings did they feel alive and together. A unity that existed no other time but now. They were just finishing up a wild bout of laughter prompted by Corcha's reminiscences of life during the rule of the Roman Empire by the Caesars.

"—and the entire room would be filled with every imagined food and drink so that no taste would go undiscovered. They would feast and they would feast and they would feast." A giggle started around the circle of women as they watched Corcha's animated face, her eyes getting wider and wider with her talk of eating. "And they would feast! Until they could stand no more! Then they would go into another room specifically for the purpose of throwing up!" Several of the women groaned in mock sickness as they imagined the room filled with vomiting Romans. Their laughter increased as the absurdity of the entire event sank in as Corcha went on. "As soon as their discomfort passed, they returned to the first room and they would feast, and they would feast—" Again the Maulkians exploded into laughter.

"That's as bad as watching Henry the Eighth's court eating their dinner!" quipped Mazinna, her remark again stimulating the laughter.

"Oh, but even better, my sisters, were the orgies of the Romans—especially under Caligula and Nero."

"Now that sounds interesting!" leered Essadora as the others stepped up their giggling and laughter once again. She grinned, leaning forward, her chin resting in the palm of her hand. "Think of having an entire room full of men and you'd get to sample each one in a single night. Sounds like a superb time-saving device to me!"

"Since when are you worried about saving time?" laughed Braneesa.

"The thought of having all those willing males in one room is what I find appealing," added Washka.

"You wouldn't know what to do with a single man, let alone a whole room full," smirked Essadora.

"Ooooh, bitchy, bitchy, bitchy," teased Fleena.

"Essadora would probably reverse the Roman order," Hatisha said as she joined in the humor. "She'd eat the men and make love to the food!"

Essadora leaned back in her chair. "At least I'd do it deliciously!" Her sensual delivery was not lost on the group and they again burst into laughter.

"Essadora, you're so wicked," chimed Washka and Fleena together.

"Essadora's trademark," Corcha commented, grinning.

"Among other things," interjected Tamara.

"Yes, some of us are lucky enough to have a personality to draw from." A patronizing smile graced Essadora's lips.

"And then there are those who have to fake it," Tamara said, smirking.

"What was it you were saying earlier, Hatisha, about the male witches of Transylvania?" asked Mazinna, skillfully changing the subject.

"They weren't exactly witches, more a nightmare turned real," began Hatisha, grateful for Mazinna's quick action. The last thing they needed before the Eve was Essadora and Tamara cutting at one another. "When I was a young girl, a Maulkian male called Nuhannd found himself smitten by a young mortal woman."

"A mortal? Back when females were so plentiful? Ugh!"

"But the young woman had no desire for the witch," continued Hatisha.

"Oh, please! You do jest!"

"What was wrong with her? Was she dead?"

"Dead and buried!"

"Embalmed!"

"What else could you expect from a mortal?"

"She had no designs on the male, for her heart had been broken by the death of her twin brother during a hunting trip." Washka and Fleena joined hands. Their sadness indicated they knew how she must have felt.

"Nuhannd would not be dissuaded. He performed magic for her, made her family want for nothing, and spoke to her in poems of love, but she would only cry and gather flowers for her brother's grave."

"He should have made love to her; that would have changed her foolishness!"

"Maybe not. I understand that many mortals don't even *like* sex."

"Not like it? Now I've heard it all!"

"For not liking it, their numbers prove they endure a lot of it!" Everyone laughed.

"How altruistic of them!"

"Nuhannd decided the only way to win her was to bring her brother back."

"Hadn't the mortal been dead past the time?"

"Yes, true, he was past the time a Maulkian can save a mortal. But Nuhannd was determined.

"Through research and speculation, he decided that it was possible to raise the dead by injecting blood into the body."

"Nevermind the blood, I know how he could have injected life into me."

"One can tell the Eve is near," commented Hatisha, "all of you are as lustful as I've ever seen you! One can't even tell a straight story."

"Oh, please go on Hatisha."

"So what did our love-sick male finally do?" queried Essadora.

"He decided that the arteries in the neck and the leg were the best entry points; with the neck the more readily accessible. By magically extending his canine teeth, past his front incisors, he had the perfect tools for not only piercing the skin, but also transporting the blood from his body into the dead man's. Nuhannd went to the grave after dark, knowing he would not be seen. For three nights he visited the grave and removed the dirt by magic. Lifting the body in his arms, he would sink his teeth into the brother's neck, passing along his Maulkian blood until he felt weak. The body would then be returned to the coffin, the grave covered, and Nuhannd would return home to rest.

"When he returned on the fourth night, however, Nuhannd found the grave empty. But the body hadn't been stolen, it had dug itself out!"

"Dug itself?"

"No!"

"What made him think that?"

"Because the earth around the grave had been tunneled out."

"What did he do?"

"He went to the young woman to see if the brother had gone there."

"And?" they cried in unison, knowing Hatisha's penchant for theatrics.

"The brother was not there, but he had been there. He had attacked his loving sister and drained all the blood from her body through *his* canine teeth—exactly the opposite of what Nuhannd had done to bring him alive. This new creature—for he was no longer mortal—could only sustain his life by drinking the blood from live victims!"

"Ugh!" Mazinna said, with a distasteful look on her face, "the thought turns my stomach."

"Before the night was over, the creature had claimed three more victims. Nuhannd was beside himself at the death of his love and was not aware of the terrible menace he had allowed to roam free. Night after night, the creature would claim more victims while Nuhannd sat in his misery, mourning his loss. The mortal peasants armed themselves as best they could, but the menace was growing in giant proportions because the creature would return to his victims' graves for three nights until they, too, had joined him in his nocturnal quest.

"This is where the mortal legends of 'vampires' originated. The creature was named for the bat that is known for sucking the blood of animals. The small village that we lived near was rapidly dwindling in population and they came to us for help. Their fear was great for them to seek us out. For even as early as then, they were beginning to treat us as if we were a disease in need of extermination.

"We gathered our people together to talk of the subject and what could be done. We were at a disadvantage, for the vampires never approached us, knowing our powers to be greater than theirs. As we discussed the method in which the vampires killed, Nuhannd seemed to break out of a deep sleep. Sobbing, he told us of his experiment of trying to bring the mortal back to life: he had just realized that he was the cause of his sweetheart's death.

"Since the vampires were nocturnal creatures, it was decided that it would be best to find them during the light of day. Their numbers were great and to this day I cannot be sure that we managed to get them all."

"You mean those *things* still exist?"

"Might exist. I am not certain. I have not encountered one since."

"Why am I not comforted by that." Corcha's remark was not a question.

"Whatever became of Nuhannd?" asked Sarinda.

"He was so overcome by what had happened, he left us and we never saw him again."

"All for the love of a lowly mortal," sniffed Essadora.

"For love, period," corrected Tamara, whose sober look kept Essadora from firing off any retort.

The entire group became lost in their own thoughts and it was several minutes before anyone chose to speak.

"How many mortals," began Essadora with her concentration focused on the braiding and unbraiding of her hair, "does it take to make ice cubes?"

"Oh, no! Not again! Forget it!" yelled everyone at once, breaking the somber mood.

"How many?" asked Sarinda earnestly.

"Don't encourage her!" blurted Hatisha in the middle of sipping her wine. "We'll have to listen to her all night if you do."

Essadora just grinned nastily without taking her eyes from the rhythmic movements of her hands.

• • •

David sat in his car smoking a cigarette. His mind wandered aimlessly from subject to subject as he waited for the library to close. He could see the lights going out one by one as the librarian moved from the back bookstacks toward the front. David had told her they were off for tonight, but everything had gone so well with Larry, he decided to treat himself to a little dessert.

He rolled down the window as the librarian locked the door. He liked watching her move; when she wasn't nervous, she was graceful, fluid motion.

"Hey!" he called, startling her. David climbed out of his car and went to her, surrounding her with his strong arms.

"You scared me!" she said, shaken.

"I'm sorry, baby," he murmured into her ear as he snuggled her.

"You said you weren't feeling well!" She was very upset, which allowed her to be cold toward him in a way she had never thought possible before.

"What can I say? I just couldn't get you out of my mind. I had to see you." His tongue circled her ear lobe as he pulled her closer to him, wanting her to feel his need pressing against the restricting fabric of his pants.

"Well, I'm not in the mood now!" She started moving toward her car, but David held her still.

"I can get you in the mood, baby. What do you say?"

"I don't like being pulled back and forth. Sometimes I feel as if you're making fun of me!" she pouted.

"You're right." He released her. "I'm sorry. I haven't been fair with you lately. I've just had so much on my mind—I know that's no excuse—but I wanted you to know I've been thinking about you." He headed to his car. "Good night, babe." He was betting his hand wouldn't even make the door handle. It didn't.

"David?"

"Yeah, babe?" He kept his smile hidden as he turned. She shyly went to him and gave him a peck on the cheek. He opened his car door for her and she got in with David close behind. Once inside, he locked the door and scooted to her side as he began kissing her.

"David? David?" she breathed between kisses, "aren't we going to go to my place?"

"What's wrong with here?" He slid his hand up the back of her blouse, undoing the buttons as he went.

"Someone might see us." She tried to intercept his wandering hands.

"Then, they'll get an education." He began biting her neck tenderly as he pulled her blouse outside her skirt.

"David!" She swatted his arm as his hand went inside her bra. He pulled back roughly and put his arms on the back of the seat as he stared at the library.

"Get out," he said coldly.

"Get out?" She just sat there looking at him, her blouse down around her forearms.

"You heard me."

"I—I'm sorry," she stammered, "I just didn't—I mean, you're married. Aren't you afraid of your wife's finding out?"

"Don't you think she knows?" His look was agitated. "She doesn't want to give me what I need, she'd rather someone else take care of me so she won't have to bother. So I come here looking for a little love and understanding, and what do I get? 'David don't!' "

Without pause, she put her arms around his neck and hugged him. "I'm sorry."

"No you're not. You don't care. Women are all the same."

"But I do love you!" She protested with just the amount of emotion that David was waiting for.

"Then do me—right here." He began to unbutton his pants.

"Can't we go to my place first?" She looked sweet and appealing.

"I want it right here." He moved his pants down and she began without further protest. David leaned his head back on the top of the seat and closed his eyes. He pretended it was Tamara who was with him. Her mouth. Her hands. It was luscious Tamara who was building him to his explosion. Her, filling his every need. And one day, he promised himself, it would be her. It would be all or nothing.

The rain pounded Richard as he ran through the night. He was being chased. The trees and bushes slashed at his face and arms as he continued on. Every few steps he would cast a wary glance over his shoulders trying to spot the thing that he was afraid of, but he could only hear the thunder as jolts of lightning licked the black sky.

Richard stumbled. He lost his camera. Getting up quickly, he pushed onward. A light danced through the trees ahead and he made for it with a new determination. A sharp branch tore his shirt half off him as mud, leaves, and his own hair got into his eyes. The light was closer. Growing bigger. He stepped wrong and turned his knee, sending him to the ground in pain. He began crawling. He couldn't let the thing get him.

The light was from a window of a small house and Richard called out, but the thunder drowned him out. He tried to rise, but he fell against the door, causing it to burst open into a warm, well-lit room. He was sprawled on the floor, trying to grasp where he was, when the door shut and the wind, rain, and thunder were locked outside.

A dark-haired woman slipped her arms around his shoulders and helped him to the bed by the hearth. A soft towel blotted his face. She undid his jeans and slipped them from him before examining his leg. She removed his shirt and placed it in front of the hearth beside his pants. He closed his eyes for a moment and felt her place two blankets over him. He was starting to feel warmer already.

Opening his eyes, he looked at his surroundings. It was a one-room cabin with a hearth, two windows opposite each other and a door. The kitchen consisted of a sink, oven, a small table with two chairs, and a hand pump at the sink.

The woman was filling a bowl with soup from a kettle bubbling over the hearth. She carefully brought it to the small table beside the bed and set it down before getting a spoon. She helped Richard sit up and she stuffed pillows and a rolled up blanket behind him before settling alongside, facing him. Carefully, she began dipping the spoon in the soup and brought it to Richard's mouth. Every time he tried to ask a question about her or where he was, she shoved a spoon in his mouth. Since he wasn't allowed to talk, he contented himself with watching her beautiful, dark eyes and long flowing hair. She looked out of place in this cabin, as if she had been born to more.

The soup finished, the woman put everything away and began extinguishing the lanterns. Only the light from the hearth filled the warm, cozy room as the storm raged on outside. Richard was lying flat again and he noticed that his knee wasn't throbbing anymore. The woman appeared at his bedside and he turned to look at her. She was naked. She lifted the blankets and climbed into the narrow, wood frame bed with him. She was deliciously warm and soft, her hair brushing his arm and shoulder as she pulled herself up and on his body. Her full breasts pressed against him, sending waves of pleasure coursing through him. Her lips brushed his gently, her warm breath tickling them slightly. His arms went around her as she held his shoulders. Their mouths met in a passionate thirst.

Thunder exploded within the room, setting everything on fire. The woman was gone as Richard struggled to get out of bed. The thing that had been chasing him filled the doorway. His body was trapped inside the blankets as he fell from the bed, crawling to the opposite side of the room as the dark figure bore down on him.

Richard jerked awake. The darkness of the room was relieved every few seconds as the lightning flashed. Paul slept in the bed next to Richard's, the covers over his head. The thunder rumbled again. It had been a dream. It had been some time since he had experienced one that intense. He rolled over and pulled the covers up higher, even though it was still very warm in the room despite the rain.

"Where are thee?" Hatisha placed her hand on her daughter's as she appraised Tamara's faraway look. Her attention returned to the group and Tamara smiled.

"I was just thinking that this unquenchable thirst that overcomes us at this time seems to affect the mortals as well."

"Truly you are right, my sister," began Fleena animatedly. "I counted several mortal couples sneaking into the cornfields today."

"My, my, it doesn't take much to engage your interest." Essadora smirked.

"I was simply agreeing with Tamara."

"I rest my case."

"You'll have to pardon Essadora, Fleena. She gets this way when she can't get a man to love her. She's so sour, they're afraid it would be like making love to a lemon, a frozen lemon," Tamara chided, causing the group to giggle.

Essadora sat up straight in her chair, her eyes narrowing at Tamara. "I can understand your jealousy, Tamara," she began haughtily, "since you can only get a boy to make love to you."

Tamara grinned as she met Essadora's look. "You're green because what takes your men all night to do, mine does all night!"

The group hooted.

"All these sexual barbs make me hunger for a cigarette," deadpanned Corcha, completely exploding the group into laughter. "It's too bad witches don't smoke," she added.

"I'd say Essadora's doing a rather nice imitation!"

"Sweet sister," Essadora began with a honey voice, "my fondest wish for you would be that all your children look like me!"

Larry Caylin sat on his bed in the dark, fully dressed, as he thought about David's offer. "You can be in charge of Trent's destruction, and I'll take care of *her*." Goose bumps raised on his arms and he began rubbing his neck to loosen the tension. He had led his friend Bobby to believe that he had put aside any plans of getting Jesse, and he felt guilty. He had never lied to Bobby before. Bobby just didn't understand, he assured himself.

Larry had been raised to compete. His daddy was headstrong and unforgiving when it came to losing. "No son of mine is gonna be a loser!" his daddy repeated over and over again inside Larry's head. It didn't matter if it was sports, school, or life—Larry had to come out on top. Every school his team played would be crushed by Larry's team, every one except Brentwood. It also was no mystery that Jesse was the keystone to every sports team he played on. As soon as Jesse had left for college, Brentwood became average in the competitive field. They actually suffered losses for the first time in four years. Larry's daddy would approach his son after every game against Brentwood with the same accusatory look. "How could you let that bastard get away with that?" he'd rant.

Larry had always tried harder than humanly possible to best Jesse, but he couldn't. That was why Jesse had to be stopped. Because he obviously wasn't human. He made everything look too damned easy. Even in school. The guy was always done first! He never seemed to labor over homework. All the teachers liked him. And the girls, especially the girls. They were all crazy about him. It really irked Larry when he recalled that Jesse never showed any emotion other than friendliness toward them. He could have his pick of the lot—and he didn't even want any of them!

Larry slammed his fist into the palm of his other hand. Bastard! Bastard! was all he could repeat to himself. Jesse Trent's days were numbered.

"—I had met them just after escaping from the convent." Mazinna paused to sip her wine. "They had the cutest little girl and we became fast friends. I hadn't been sure I even wanted to approach people, but I was so tired and hungry, it became difficult to stay distant."

"Especially if you were not yet fully acquainted with your powers, as you say," affirmed Hatisha.

"It would be several years more before I began to discover just what I was capable of. In the meantime, the family took me in and I helped around the house and tutored their daughter in exchange for my keep. Some time later, a group of people came through the nearby village and pitched their tents and unharnessed their wagons as they settled in. The family told me that the people were gypsies and they would put on shows after nightfall. Ginny, the little one I was tutoring, was beside herself with excitement, telling me that they could tell the future or make potions to ease pain or bring love. Her family never failed to visit the gypsy camp whenever they were nearby.

"I was amazed by their gaiety and abandon. They seemed to love life and were a happier lot than any mortals I have experienced since then. Their women were beautiful. They dressed in bright colors, wore yards of necklaces and jewelry, their hair was full and long, sometimes trailing below their waists. And they danced. I've never seen such dancing; their feet bare, their skirts flying, their bodies moving sensually with the music.

"Their men were not surpassed by the beauty of the women, not at all! I had never seen such dark, intelligent eyes and dark skin outside of court, when the ambassadors would come to call on King Henry. They played instruments, juggled things, played with fire, and they danced too. It was very exciting to watch them dancing so close to their women, running their hands over their bodies in a teasing fashion without ever really touching them. The crowd loved it, urging them on as they threw coins at the dancers' feet.

"Ginny pulled me away from the dancers and I followed her to a weathered-looking wagon with stairs leading up and in, a light burning from a lantern that hung from the center beam of the interior. A woman, whose looks could rival Hatisha's"—Mazinna grinned at the eldest witch—"sat at a table reading cards."

"She was a beauty, I take it," smirked Hatisha, smoothing down her hair. Everyone hooted again.

"When we entered, she looked straight up into my eyes for several, very long seconds. Ginny didn't notice; she plopped herself down to have her fortune read. The old woman looked at the child for a moment before returning her eyes to me. She nodded, almost in understanding, and went on to shuffle the cards for Ginny. She told Ginny everything she wanted to hear; how she would meet the man of her dreams, have several children and live a long, happy life. When Ginny hopped down, the old woman volunteered to read for me. I told her no thank you and turned to leave when she grabbed my hand. She looked at me very seriously before telling me that I was not alone. I never knew what she meant until I met Hatisha." Several of the witches nodded seriously.

"As we wandered through the camp I noticed a handsome gypsy male seemed to follow me with his eyes everywhere that I went. The hour was late, Ginny was in my arms asleep, as the family headed home. We had walked to the camp because the weather had been so beautiful, the night sky filled with more stars than it needed, and we knew we needed the exercise after our filling supper. The year had been a good one for the little family; they couldn't have been happier.

"I barely remember the walk home for I felt as if we were being followed. I tucked Ginny in and said good night to her parents before they went to bed. I waited for several minutes until I was sure they were asleep before I slipped quietly out the front door. I didn't even have to search for him, he stepped out of the trees as soon as I emerged from the house.

" 'Why have you come here?' I asked as soon as I was away from the house. He extended his hand to me while motioning with his other to be quiet. I was trembling as I took his hand and it confused me, for the night was warm and I hadn't felt a chill. We walked several yards into the woods before he leaned me against the trunk of a tree so tall, I could not see its top.

"I had not been with anyone before that time, but I have since discovered that I was being initiated by a very skilled lover. His lips were warm and inviting, his hands skilled—"

"From diligent practice, no doubt!" mused Corcha.

"Yes," smiled Mazinna shyly. "At this time, I had not taken on my robes of color, instead I wore a simple skirt and blouse, which presented absolutely no obstacle for him. I thought the beauty of that night would live with me forever, but I was wrong. Some time passed and I discovered that I was with child. Ginny's parents were not at all understanding; they threw me out. The wife even accused the husband of the deed. I was so hurt and angry at their treatment of me that I told the wife she was correct. I could hear them screaming at one another for quite a distance as I journeyed through the forest."

Mazinna finished her wine and Hatisha refilled it for her. No one spoke, but waited patiently for her to continue, sensing that there was more she wanted to tell.

"I lost the child. I was alone. Living in the dirt and moss. I swore that I would never go near people again. I lived alone for many, many years before I heard talk of a new world having been discovered. I thought to myself, how wonderful it must be to live in a place and not run into anyone for miles!"

"It must have been quite an awakening to reach the coast of the new world, only to find it mobbed with mortals!"

"Here! Here!" agreed the others, banging on the table.

"Yes, indeed," smiled Mazinna, remembering. "It has

only been since finding all of you and settling here that I have felt good about myself. And about the mortals."

"Now let's not go overboard, Mazinna," muttered Essadora as she changed her position.

Corcha began to giggle, but the others could tell it was not over what Essadora had said.

"Well, don't just sit there, share the joke!"

"I was just thinking," Corcha began with a wicked smile, "the mortal who seduced Mazinna must have thought he was really something, I mean, following her home and taking her virginity, enjoying the greatest pleasures he'd ever known—probably thinking it was all his skill—only to discover later that he was now forever saddled with the Witches' Curse!"

"Ah! That's right!" said Fleena and Washka, respectively, laughing at the vision of the male unable to be satisfied by a mere mortal female ever again.

"And what of you, Essadora? What tales of intrigue do you hide in your closet that you never share with us? Or are you only capable of wisecracks?" questioned Hatisha.

"I never share my experiences, sweet witch, for I know this group to be faint of heart!"

"Ooooooh! Liar! That will be the day!" Everyone had a retort for Essadora's smugness. "You wish! Please!"

"Soon we will have to levitate the table, so thick will the bullsh—"

"Be a sport, Essadora. Tell us an adventure," urged Hatisha, interrupting Tamara.

"Unlike the rest of you, I do not derive a great deal of pleasure dwelling on the mortals as you do."

Jesse looked out of his window as he leaned against the sill. He was naked, trying to stay cool as he watched the mist hanging in the air. His look wandered back to his room and his night vision allowed him to make out its furnishings and effects situated about him.

He wondered where he and Tamara would live after the ceremony. Jesse supposed they would live with Hatisha, but he wasn't sure if they'd be comfortable there. All right, he admitted to himself, he wouldn't feel comfortable there. He was looking forward to making love with Tamara every night, and the thought of Hatisha being aware of that made him nervous. It then dawned on him that the old witch was very capable of knowing when they made love any time she felt like it! He smiled. Boy, how different his life would be after this weekend!

He thought of his parents and how good they had been to him. How they hadn't even argued with him when he announced he wasn't going back to school. Since he had been with Tamara, they had pretty much gone along with whatever decisions he made. One thing that was particularly gratifying about becoming a witch was it would allow him to take care of his parents in their old age—which if they followed the normal course for Brentwood, could be another sixty to seventy years!

Crossing to his bed, Jesse laid down and stared at the ceiling. His thoughts idled for a few moments until his ex-girlfriend, Lyndie, came to mind. He had run across her with one of her friends on his walk to town from the hill where Tamara had left him. He felt guilty that he couldn't muster a single emotion about her, not even fondness for their time together before he'd known Tamara. That old life seemed vague and unreal.

His thoughts returned to his warm dark room and his sleepy eyes convinced Jesse to climb under his sheets while he waited for Tamara. Lyndie was a million years ago, he told himself, a million, zillion years.

''Don't let this witch fly home, okay?'' quipped Tamara as Mazinna accidentally knocked over her wine glass. The others giggled, enjoying the silliness the usually sober Tamara was displaying.

Though Sarinda felt happy, she began to think of David. He hadn't arrived home before she had left. She reached out with her senses, but knew he would not be there. At least not in Brentwood. Sarinda knew all about the librarian. And the secretary. And all the others. At first she had thought to scare them away, but she knew he would only find more. Why couldn't she have been like Tamara? Maybe he would have loved her then. At least if she had been more like Tamara, he wouldn't have dared to insult her this way.

David had grown up in Brentwood and had always been

different from everyone else. From the first, he had seemed out of place in the country. It was as if he were from the city and had been mysteriously transplanted in this small town he referred to as "Nowhere Land." It was always believed he would leave Brentwood as soon as he was able—so it was quite a surprise when he decided to stay. He did leave long enough to attend Butler College, but since he was only away at school, the Maulkians had not erased his memory. It was forbidden for the townspeople to discuss the 'witches' with nonbelievers, but it was not a problem when kids went off to school, for they knew they would be viewed as crazy fools if they told outsiders that Brentwood was filled with real, live witches. David never discussed the witches with outsiders and he returned to Brentwood, settling down and becoming a writer. Other than his philandering, he was a model citizen and the rest of the townspeople seemed charmed by his blue eyes and diplomatic ways. The witches ignored him as just another mortal, until he started boldly approaching Tamara.

It had been a beautiful spring day. Tamara had settled among the grass and dandelions that lay between the cornfields, and she closed her eyes as the sun warmed her upturned face. Suddenly, she sensed she was not alone. Opening her eyes, she watched David approaching her from across the field. It was utterly unthinkable that a mere mortal would accost her so. If he had been an ignorant outsider then there would have been no insult—but this was inexcusable. If he wanted something, he had only to approach the speaker, Jonathan Webster, who would speak to Hatisha. That was how things were done, and had always been done, for the last two hundred years.

"Hello, Tamara," he smiled. When she didn't speak, he sat down in front of her. Her cold, wary look told him that he was walking a shaky tightrope without a net to catch him. "I know I'm not supposed to speak to you unless you speak to me first," he began in a respectful voice that kept Tamara's temper reined in, "but I find that what I have to say should only be heard by you and not shared through a grapevine of communications."

Tamara rose, her stern, resentful look clearly explaining to him what she thought of his opinion of their tried-and-true communication system. He rose quickly, trying to express his humility and his awareness of how out-of-line he was.

"I don't mean to be disrespectful, and I don't want to make you angry—please allow me to tell you what I need to say." She continued to glare at him with her haughty, piercing look, but since she did not move, he took that as a silent consent for him to go on. He dropped to his knees as he continued to look into her eyes, his face the perfect picture of devotion. "I'm in love with you, Tamara. I want nothing more in the world than to be at your side, loving you, trying my best to make you happy."

The absurdity of the situation kept her anger in check. She had planned not to speak to him, thereby showing him that she had not approved of his boldness, thus invalidating all that he would say to her. But now, as his words echoed in the stillness around them, she could not let this go unreproached.

"Mortal," she began, the danger in her voice alerting him to the severity of his transgression, "thee dost not care so much for me as for what thee thinks the marrying of a witch could bring!"

"No, really Tamara!"

She began turning to pure radiance before him, the twinkling lights enveloping her from head to toe.

"No, don't go!" David reached within the radiance and touched her robe. Immediately the twinkling ceased, and Tamara glared at David with burning red eyes.

"Thou has insulted me for the last time." With a wave of her hand, David disappeared from her sight and found himself in the town square—completely naked! Tamara smiled with satisfaction as she used her inner eye to watch David hurrying through town to get back to his room at the boarding house. His sudden appearance in such an embarrassing condition left no doubt in the minds of the townspeople that David had made one of the witches angry, and they laughed about it for days.

The next time David approached a witch, he chose more carefully. He knew that Sarinda seemed to be the "runt" of the witch litter, and though she was quite beautiful she could not measure up to her sisters. She would be easier to manipulate. He arranged to make Sarinda begin their conversation by coming daily to her favorite place by a brook, so that she couldn't use it herself without addressing him. It was an unexpected bonus when he discovered that Sarinda had always worshipped him from afar.

So instead of the conflict of trying to get acquainted with her, he only had to deal with the witches' prejudice against marrying mortals. David had never been a more ardent lover in his life. There wasn't anything he wasn't prepared to do for Sarinda. He counted himself lucky that Sarinda wasn't too demanding, for it was his ambition that moved him, rather than his heart.

The witches had no qualms about bedding down with a mortal, you just didn't mate with one for life. Somehow, David had to convince a vacillating Sarinda that he was right and her sisters were wrong. He had never seen a male witch in the town of Brentwood, so he had deduced that they were the stronger and couldn't be bothered with staying in one place too long. In marrying Sarinda, he would be initiated as a witch and then be in the same class as Tamara. An equal. Then she would see what she had passed up by ignoring him. Then it would be time for retribution.

But the joke was on David, for after all his scheming to marry Sarinda, he was a witch in name only, and now was saddled with a wife he didn't want.

Sarinda was so lost in her thoughts that she didn't realize she had asked a question until she heard the low gasp and looked up to see them all staring at her.

"Why are there mortals?" Hatisha repeated Sarinda's soft question in her usual calm tone. The others seemed to hold their breath as they glanced between Sarinda and Hatisha, waiting to see what the eldest witch would do.

Maybe it was the wine. Maybe it was because Sarinda, the weakest of all, had asked. Or maybe Hatisha felt her time was limited on this earth, and someone . . . someone should know. She was the keeper of knowledge since she was the eldest true Maulkian. It was her job to pass what she knew to the younger generation anyway. So why not now, while they were all still together, still alive? Hatisha had felt the creeping darkness for some time. She wanted to tell the story.

"We did not come from this world. Our planet is long dead and far away." As she spoke, Hatisha moved her hand around in a circle at the center of the table. When she withdrew her hand, a hologram figure of a planet hovered above the table. The planet resembled earth, except that the land masses were smaller, more numerous, and sprinkled across its seas. Their entire history began to play before the witches' eyes as the hologram characters performed Hatisha's story.

"On Maulkian, what we do here in secret was open and natural for us. Our powers were encouraged and reinforced by our parents. A council of the Elders guided us with sound decisions, and life was good." Hatisha smiled at the memories as they appeared in the center of the table. "We even flew through the skies like birds—we were the masters of the skies! And to this day I still cannot fathom how the mortals ever came up with the idea that witches needed broomsticks!" A burst of laughter released their tension, and the witches leaned forward eagerly to hear more.

"We were not a warring race; we minded our own business, and life was good. We believed our powers to be limitless. The skies were clear and bright, and the Maulkian sun with its five discernible points nourished our bodies and gave us our powers. We did not have the technology that the mortals now possess, having relied so much on our own powers for whatever we wanted, but we had all that we needed to survive and be happy. That was enough.

"Unfortunately, life does not always continue in storybook fashion and one day our lives were changed forever. A strange shelter that we later learned to call 'spaceship' landed in our fields. Having never known creatures other than ourselves, we had no idea what we should do or how we should behave. Never having known fear, we approached the shelter bearing gifts of welcome. But when the doors opened, hideous creatures the like of which we could never have dreamt of in our worst nightmares burst out and began slaughtering us. They were seven feet tall, with horns and claws, muscled bodies, and huge wings that jutted out from their shoulder blades and shielded them from our magic. Their eyes were black and empty. Beneath their clothing of leather and furs, long, dark hair covered their hips, loins and legs. Their feet were hooved, and they had long, menacing tails." As the hologram of the Devilin appeared, the witches gasped in horror.

"Their attack was so sudden, so ruthless, panic was the only thing we knew. We scattered and ran, forgetting our powers, the fear in our breasts more powerful than our logic. The creatures were more than just fierce brutes, they also possessed the same powers as we. But it was their aggression alone that overcame us. They slaughtered our men and raped our women. We were thousands in the hills that overlooked our city; they were but a few, yet they feasted on our food and made themselves comfortable in our homes."

Hatisha paused to sip her wine as everyone in the circle waited breathlessly for her to continue.

"While the enemy slept in our city, and despite objections from the men, the Elders held council in the woods with some of the women of our species. The Elders told of a special way of killing the enemy by turning their own power against them. Throughout the night, the chosen women practiced the chant silently as the rest of the women and the men watched from a distance. The chant was said to be so powerful that no one must ever use it, for it brings instant death. Since that time we have never uttered a chant out loud, in memorial of that dark night.

"When the Maulkian sun rose, the females were waiting outside the city gates for the enemy to claim them. Our women have always been blessed with beauty and grace, irresistible to any man they chose; the invaders would never turn them down. The volunteers consisted of the women who had been raped, or those whose husbands had been murdered; they wanted revenge. The invaders were not even suspicious; they thought it only fitting that the women serve them and their appetites, for they were the conquerors. We watched the volunteers disappear into the city. To us who waited in the hills, it seemed an eternity would pass before this would end. Our men were not happy with the plan, but they remained quiet as they wondered what the women had been told to do. You could hear the grass gently moving in the fields as the Maulkian sun climbed higher over our heads.

"Then, it rose, like a siren from the black side of hell, the unmistakable sound of dying. The screams of the enemy echoed throughout the city, and our breath caught at the sound of the icy shrills.

"Slowly, one by one, each woman emerged from the city carrying a container. Each vessel held the ashes that were all that remained of the invaders, and these were presented to the Elders as instructed. The Elders planned to study the remains and record the horror as a warning to future generations of our kind.

"We were still in shock, everyone wandering around, some returning to their homes. No one quite seemed to know what to do. It was then that Tachmann stepped forward to organize and lead us. Though I was very young, I remember well his charisma, his rugged, handsome looks, his booming voice ordering us about. The Elders nodded their heads in approval at his lead. He seemed to bring back life to our souls." The witches murmured at the handsome hologram of the male witch.

"It was Tachmann who led several men into the strange flying shelter. Inside was a marvel of lights and machinery that seemed to have no beginning or end. And tied to the control panel, barely alive, was a poor tortured creature. His pale, thin body was like the Earth insect we call the Praying Mantis, but he was like us in spirit. We healed him and treated him well, feeling kinship after fighting the same enemy. He was an extremely intelligent being known as a Nuballin. His gentleness and quiet manner endeared him to us and he gladly told us of his world and how the spaceship had come to Maulkian.

"Nuballins had been raiding the planet of Devilin for generations. The Devilins, as we had discovered to our sorrow, were fierce and war-like, bred on Devilin by the Nuballins for slave labor. To keep their population low, every few cycles the Nuballins would capture hundreds of the creatures with special collars that prevented the Devilins from using their magic. They would then transport them to their planet to be used for the manpower that the Nuballins lacked, since they had concentrated on developing their mental powers.

"On this particular trip, however, things had not gone according to plan. Somehow, the Devilins had broken free of their confinement and had killed everyone except our friend. They did not want to return to Devilin for fear of being recaptured, so they forced their captive to take them to the nearest hospitable planet. Unfortunately, that planet was Maulkian.

"As time went by and our new friend recovered his strength, we all returned to our previous lifestyles, with a few exceptions. Male Maulkians have always been unable to father children at any time other than the Eve and the Holy Day. Now, with many of our males dead, it became top priority to breed new males. The women outnumbered the men fifteen to one, and the women were always fertile, so we hoped soon to be able to put this tragedy behind us.

"But this was not to be. We soon began to realize that our men were avoiding the women who had caused the destruction of the enemy. For the first time, we knew fear of our own kind. No amount of encouragement could entice the men to join with them. Angry, hurt, those women moved off to live together in a small corner of the city, outcasts even among most of the other women.

"And, as if the division of our kind wasn't enough, we soon began dying."

"Dying?!" repeated Fleena, with wide, frightened eyes.

"Yes. Three weeks after the destruction of our enemy, a deadly virus that had lived passively within their bodies now flourished in us under the rays of our Maulkian sun. The same rays that gave us our powers and nourished our existence threatened to destroy us all. Everyone was hit, except for our Nuballin friend. The eldest died first, with the men seemingly most susceptible, while the women were only mildly sick. No magic, no potion, nothing worked. When a cure was finally found, we were reinfected by the food supply, or by the air around us.

"Again, it was Tachmann who stepped forward to take control of our hopeless situation. He believed that if we were to leave our planet and seek out another, the cure might take hold and we would be able to save ourselves. The Nuballin agreed and offered to take as many as his ship would hold. The Elders chose those of us who would go. After a few days of preparations, my family entered the ship with the other chosen ones and headed for the unknown. Once aboard, the cure took hold. Our people began to regain their strength. All but my father were to survive. He had been the only Elder to come with us, and he passed on to me the book which told of the winged invaders' savage assault on our people. The book also tells of the findings of the Elders' experiments on the ashes of the invaders. After I am gone you can refer to the book for the answers to any questions you may have. Until then, it shall remain in my keeping inside the altar."

"But what of our planet? And how many of us were aboard the ship? How did we come here?" The questions seemed to come from everyone as Hatisha put up her hands to call for silence before continuing.

"We believe that all who remained on Maulkian are now dead. There is a possibility that they managed to save themselves, but we will never know. Ninety-seven of us left Maulkian that day and one hundred and sixteen landed on this planet. The journey took two mortal years to complete. The Nuballin pilot had passed this planet on his journeys between Nuballin and Devilin, and said that only lower life forms existed here. The climate was also variable and since we Maulkians drew our life from our crop fields, we should be able to adjust. Tachmann asked the Nuballin to check up on us when he made his return flight from his home planet to Devilin. He also promised to check on the others left behind on Maulkian.

"We landed here over a million years ago in the middle of a lush, green forest filled with wild flowers. Earth was just as beautiful as Maulkian had been, and we danced and hugged one another at our good fortune. My mother and I, Tachmann and his family, the women who had been outcasts, and all the others who were left alive swore to carry on the legacy of our people.

"Of course, as it seems with all things, our new life was not without problems. Our powers lacked the strength we once enjoyed under the rays of the Maulkian sun. It should humble those of you at this table to know that the powers you now possess are nothing compared to those we once controlled." The witches glanced quickly at one another, some crossing their arms across their chests with the palms resting above each breast in a sign of protection. It was also a sign of yielding to a greater power.

"It was easier for the children who had been born on the journey to adjust, since they had nothing to compare it to. Some fought any changes; others, like myself, turned to the use of plants to aid our magic, and still others, like Tamara, practiced every possible technique to find the most effective way. This constant practicing and challenging of herself has made her part of the new breed of Maulkians who emerged after our landing here. They are not the most powerful witches ever to exist, but they are the most powerful this planet has known. And if she is not careful," Hatisha began with a smile, "Tamara could put an end to all of us by accident."

The circle looked to Tamara with smiles, enjoying Hatisha's teasing manner. Essadora preened her silver and brunette hair with casual efficiency, looking the perfect picture of boredom. Finally, her eyes glided up to Tamara's as she said: "You haven't told us about the mortals."

Tamara returned her haughty look. Hatisha placed her hand on Tamara's to divert her attention as she continued.

"Our arrival on earth meant new beginnings. There were only thirty males compared to eighty-six females. It was decided that, for the good of the race, the males had to be shared. Those that were married could stay with their families, but at the sunset of the Eve, each male would have to mate with as many females as possible. The race must be saved. Since that time, Maulkians have stopped mating for life. It became too hard for the families to endure. And on Earth, as it had been on Maulkian, the outcast women were left alone and unapproached, even at the height of the mating rituals.

"Filled with bitterness and resentment, those women moved off to a village of their own and took mates."

Braneesa moved uneasily in her chair, her eyes unable to meet Hatisha's when she asked her question.

"If the male witches would not mate with them . . . then who did?"

"The human race we know was born of witch and animal. *We* are the missing link that the mortals are always speaking of. Our women cast spells on themselves to become like the primitive humans of Earth, and returned to their witch form after they had mated. The offspring seemed to us half-ape and half-witch, and did not possess the same powers as the rest of us. Throughout the centuries the powers have been slowly bred out of the species as they continued to mate among themselves. They all have some powers, but they are not aware of them or don't know how to use them. They give these powers scientific labels—ESP, clairvoyance, telekinesis. Their list of names goes on and on, but every mortal is part witch. That is why the mortals have taken on their own version of the ceremonies, dress in black, cast their limited magic—they all seek the witch that is buried deep in their souls. They are the descendents of a great race and they are the bastards in our closet—to coin a mortal phrase."

"And what of the rest of our people?" Mazinna's voice trembled.

"We were so outraged by what the outcast women had done that we left to find a new place to live. It was decreed that these women with their monstrous offspring would not be allowed to live with us, share our ceremonies, or speak to us before we gave permission. We never dreamt how fast the new species would multiply or that a million years later, despite all of our powers, the mortals would become more advanced, and threaten our very existence."

Washka and Fleena took each other's hand for comfort before Fleena asked her question. "If the men came to Earth with us, then why are there none here now?"

"The men fought over who would be the leader. They fought over everything—land, food, shelter—even women. Ten women for every man, and they still fought. Finally, we could take no more, and we women banded together and threw out the men. The only time they would be allowed near us was Witches' Eve and the Holy Day, which is our mating time. When the drive takes us over at this time, the males would seek out our women, no matter how far they had to travel. It has been only recently, in the last two hundred years, that I have not seen a male witch here. I do not know if they have finally killed each other off or if they have just found other groups of our women elsewhere. I have heard rumors that our race is spread all over the face of this Earth, but I have had no desire to go out searching. It almost seems that life is better without too many of us being together in one place."

"But what of the Nuballin?" It was Sarinda who had asked.

"I know not. Tachmann speculated that he had met with trouble upon his return to his own planet. He might have never made it at all."

"And our families? How is it that most of us do not know who they were, or even what has become of them?" Corcha's lips pouted in her deep sadness as she waited for the answer.

"As our race splintered and separated, many of the witches lost touch with each other. Traditions were lost, families abandoned, and soon being a true witch was not such a desirable thing in the face of the advancing mortals. The children of the true born were not educated in their history or powers. Their art was lost. Wanting to survive among the mortals became more important than our heritage.

"By the time I had become an adult, I realized that our race was in terrible trouble, even though the mortals were still living in caves. As their population grew, we moved further and further away to avoid them. I brought Tamara and Sarinda here because it was one of the last places that mortals had not overrun, though I knew, even then, it was just a matter of time. But this was a new place, very beautiful and not as populated as the other places we had lived. And the Indians still lived as we had once done, using the land and the creatures as necessary—not hurting and destroying for no reason.

"When we stepped off the sailing vessel and moved through the town, I vowed that here I would make my stand. Here we would carve a life for ourselves with the mortals' help. And, for once, we would finally live in peace. But first we had to find a place to rest and I kept my senses tuned for our kind. Of course, as you know, Corcha was the first one to encounter us; then Mazinna; and Braneesa. As we traveled throughout the villages and countryside, each one of you joined us. Fleena and Washka were already here when we arrived, making it easier for us; Essadora joining us last. In the beginning I was appalled by everyone's lack of knowledge of just what it meant to be a Maulkian, and I have tried to teach you everything you must know. I am very proud of how well you have all done since then." Hatisha gave them all loving looks as she dissolved each hologram figure by grasping it in her hand.

"Then, this year," began Mazinna as she leaned forward, resting her arms on the table, her sober look piercing everyone's soul, "as in previous years, there will be no men. The ceremony will be just that—a ceremony. Unless we mate with a mortal, we will never have children or mates. This is it. This is the death of our kind. After we are gone, a true Maulkian Witch will be but a memory, then a legend, then a forgotten thought. No one will even know we've been here."

Hatisha bit her lip and looked at Tamara, who began tracing the wood grain in the table. She knew what she must do, but would her daughter ever forgive her?

"There is a male witch in our midst."

"Mother!" cried Tamara as she bolted up from her chair, knocking it to the floor. Though the rest were shocked and confused by the statement and Tamara's outburst, Essadora leaned forward, her eyes sharp with eagerness, waiting for Hatisha to continue.

"Jesse Trent is a Maulkian. Tamara has made him into one of us." The look of betrayal on Tamara's face made Hatisha's heart ache. "I'm sorry, my child, but they have a right to know."

Corcha righted Tamara's chair with a wave of her hand. "Sit, my sister, and tell us what your mother means by this." Tamara seated herself at the table and looked into her sisters' faces, hoping to instill her warmth and love for each of them, but also her conviction that her plans were right.

"I discovered that Jesse's grandparents were both Maulkians whose daughter mated with a mortal. As you know, Jesse is adopted by his parents. I don't know what became of his true parents. His adoptive parents knew nothing of his heritage, until I persuaded them that they must move to Brentwood. I have taught Jesse some things, but I'm saving the bulk of his education until after I take him on this Eve. I have found a way to take the mortal taint out of him. By the Holy Day, he shall be one of the most powerful Maulkians to ever live."

"But how?" came the simultaneous reply. Essadora licked her lips seductively.

"I do not wish to go into it at this time, but later I will gladly tell you of my discoveries. Perhaps everyone here will be lucky enough to find someone who is removed by only a generation from being a true Maulkian. Then you too can have mates.'' Tamara hoped that was that. She needed to go to Jesse before the dawn.

''I wondered why you were spending so much time with that mortal, when you are the one always looking down your nose at those among us who had taken mortals.'' Essadora wanted nothing more than to pick a fight with Tamara. Everyone was already stirred up by the news of the male witch, it wouldn't take much to set things against Tamara. Leaning forward on her elbows, looking at Tamara with a wicked smile, Essadora clicked her long lavender nails against one another. ''And you weren't going to tell us, were you?''

''I do not look down my nose at anyone who mates with a mortal.'' Tamara knew the cutting remark was aimed at Sarinda as a way of irritating Tamara into coming to her defense. Sarinda's animation drained from her face at Essadora's jab and she stared at her hands. ''I know that need sometimes outweighs priorities,'' Tamara continued. ''When my need has been great, I too have taken a mortal. But I wish to bear a child of our race. If I had not made my discoveries, I probably would eventually have mated with a mortal.''

''You weren't going to tell us, were you?'' Essadora repeated relentlessly.

Tamara glared at Essadora. The room was deadly quiet as Essadora slid her tongue across her white teeth, like a tiger waiting for just the right moment to strike. Tamara composed herself. She knew what Essadora wanted. She wasn't going to play into her hands.

''I don't even know if it will work. I didn't want to raise any false hopes.'' Tamara's tone dripped with honey.

''You were going to keep him for yourself.''

''No, Essadora, Tamara would not do such a thing to her sisters. It is a blessing that she has come close to such a discovery. Quit trying to stir up trouble. Of course, Tamara will be allowed to mate with Jesse first, it is her right. But afterward, we will each be able to mate with him.'' It was Washka who had come to Tamara's defense.

''Tell them the truth, I challenge thee!'' Essadora slammed her fist on the table, startling everyone. The challenge issued, Tamara must tell the truth.

"Alright." Tamara jumped up from her chair. "I had no intention of sharing Jesse with anyone!" She glared at Essadora.

"I knew it!" Essadora rose slowly, triumphantly savoring the moment. Now everyone would see that Tamara was not what they all thought she was. "I claim my right to the male, you cannot deny me!"

Quickly, Tamara held out her hand with the palm up, her eyes boring into Essadora's. Thin strands of smoke emitted from her palm and danced exotically across the table toward Essadora. The other women watched, mesmerized, as the smoke danced its way in a circle around Essadora's head and met itself at the front. Tamara closed her hand and yanked on the smoke strands like they were reins. The noose snapped closed around Essadora's throat. She began to gag as the smoke choked her tighter. Tamara wound the smoke around her hand and pulled again with all her might. Essadora, pulled by the smoke lasso, crashed to the table and slid across it to Tamara. Her color became tinged with blue as she struggled for air. Her nails clawed at the smoke around her neck in a vain attempt to free herself. Tamara leaned close, her voice low and dangerous.

"Deny you? I most certainly will! I have powers you haven't begun to dream about. You're right, I had no intention of sharing Jesse with anyone—especially not you. I have created my Maulkian, he belongs to me and no one else. And if you touch him . . . I shall kill you."

Tamara slowly straightened up, but the smoke still held Essadora like a vise. "I'm sorry, my sisters, but Jesse is mine. I'm sorry that you had to find out like this"—she leaned close to her ensnared victim for emphasis—"but Essadora was insistent." Straightening up, Tamara snapped her fingers, and the noose disintegrated; Essadora sucked in an urgent breath, relieving the blueness in her face. "I hope you will understand, my sisters, that I love Jesse. I wish to mate with him for the rest of our lives. Everyone here should consider taking a mate for eternity. It's time that we learned from our mistakes and restored our family units. Now, if you all will excuse me, I must be going." Tamara vanished before the others could speak.

Essadora was enraged. She choked out her words of fury. "I shall be your destruction! You will not escape me!"

Jabbing her hand in front of her, she twisted her fingers in to form a fist with a quick spiral movement, causing a whirlwind to engulf her in the middle of the table.

"I will have my revenge!" she screamed over the noise of her churning winds that lifted her from the table and pulled her image into a tight little triangle that disappeared with a deafening explosion, leaving the rest of the Maulkians looking at one another, not quite knowing what to say.

"Leave it to Essadora. She always has to have the last word," Hatisha said with a shake of her head, trying to ease the tension. Hatisha transported a small box to the table with a wave of her hand. She took out a long, bowled tube and placed it in front of her. The tube, partially filled with water, was appliquéd with Maulkian symbols and markings. Hatisha filled the bowl with her special herb, and lit it with the end of her finger. "Here. I think everyone needs to relax a little bit. This is my new batch."

"Hatisha?"

"Yes, child?" The old woman's eyes glittered as she prepared for the question to come.

"I love my sister, Tamara, we all do," began Braneesa tentatively. "But how are we to feel when she has her male and we still have none?"

4

JESSE STARED AT the ceiling as he lay in the darkness. Rolling to his left, he checked the luminous dial of the alarm clock. Where is Tamara? he asked himself. She was rarely late. Tonight was important. This was the last night he had to suffer through the ointment that Tamara rubbed into his skin. Actually, he didn't really suffer, the body massage was quite pleasant—hell, who was he kidding? It always aroused him to a sexual earthquake. But it was the strange tingling he felt when he woke each morning that bothered him. Tamara had assured him that what he felt was the awakening of his powers.

He rolled back over to his right side and into Tamara's arms. His breath caught quickly, a gasp of surprise escaped from his lips.

"Hello." She smiled lovingly at him.

"You keep sneaking up on me, and after I'm initiated, I'll start doing it to you!" He masked his fright with a tone of anger. Her look of sadness surprised him, and he pulled her to him.

"I'm sorry, I didn't mean to. Please don't be angry with me. I'm tired of angry people today, I've had quite enough."

She had materialized naked, her warm, smooth, satin skin so inviting. Her added look of vulnerability drove him to kiss her passionately as he rolled to his back, pulling her on top of him. His hands roamed through her hair as her hands glided over his chest and down to his stomach as she sat up on him.

Edward Trent sat up in bed. Looking around in the dark, he searched for his wife. She slept quietly beside him, lost in her own dreams. Their room was filled only with the warm darkness that tugged at his eyes, beckoning him to return to his sleep. What had he heard? Was it even a sound, or rather a feeling? He rose and stepped into the slippers his wife had given him last Christmas and headed into the hallway. There! He heard another sound. It seemed to be coming from Jesse's room. Moving quickly, he opened the door and turned on the light. Jesse sat up in bed, resting back on his elbow as he shielded his eyes from the light that blinded him. Edward squinted too.

"You all right, son?"

"Yes, sir, what's wrong?"

"I heard somethin'. I thought that you were hurt—or up movin' around." Edward looked around his son's room. Nothing was out of place. The trophies were all lined in a row. The sports paraphernalia still decorated every wall. His clothes were piled on the floor the way Jesse always dumped them. So why did the elder Trent feel as though something was amiss?

"You're okay, then?"

"Yeah, I'm fine. At least I am now. I had a bad dream. Shook me up pretty good. I probably yelled out in my sleep. Sorry."

"No . . . it's alright. Good night, son."

The elder Trent looked once more around before turning off the light and shutting the door. He stood listening. It wasn't that he distrusted his son, no; Jesse had always been a good boy. But ever since Jesse had been chosen by the witch everything had been different. It was not something openly discussed in Brentwood, not bantered about at the market square like the weather, but everyone knew. And they talked about it privately, in little hushed tones. Jesse hadn't just been bedded by the witch, he had been *chosen*. Many over the years had gone to the witches' pleasure; it was considered an honor, only to have the witches erase their memories of the encounter—no one knew why. The witches also never disrupted families by choosing married men, or taking a man against his will. True, they ruled over the town, but not without the compliance of Brentwood. The crops had always been good, excluding this season, the weather never too extreme—unless it was near the

Eve. And mostly everyone in Brentwood was comfortable and happy. The witches had lived in Brentwood for better than two hundred years. They were a way of life. What would the town do without them? Yes, Jesse had been chosen, but most important, he had been chosen by the most powerful witch of the coven—Tamara. She was the most mysterious, thus the most awesome witch. Never cruel, but never warm. She stayed away from the townspeople, rarely, if ever, spoke to them, and it was well-known that it was not the witches' way to take mortals as mates, least of all Tamara, and yet she had selected Jesse. Why? He had never dared to ask Jesse, deciding that not only was it none of his business, but he had begun to think of Jesse with the same reverence that was always held toward the witches. It hurt just a little to know that Jesse wasn't really his blood. He was never able to father children. He and Margaret had spent most of their marriage trying. Although it was suggested that the witches could help them, Edward refused and they had turned to adoption. Edward had taken quickly to the small child and had reveled in all of his accomplishments. At an early age, he had seemed to excel in all that he had chosen to do. No father could be more proud. Edward had always felt that the child was gifted, but now that the witch had chosen him, Edward began to wonder if Jesse wasn't something more. Maybe he was—He shook his head. It didn't matter. He still loved his son, and Jesse seemed to be very happy about the whole thing. Leave it be and go back to bed, thought Edward to himself. He padded quietly back to his room and closed the door.

Tamara, still straddling Jesse, removed her hand from his mouth and replaced it with her lips. After the kiss she slid off of Jesse to his side.

"You almost spoke too soon. He was still listening at the door."

She smiled lovingly at him again.

"I really love the way you can appear and disappear like that. That's probably one of the first things I'm going to try after the Eve."

Tamara's look grew distant. He felt so unsure of himself with her. He never seemed to know exactly what was going on inside of her. He was sure she loved him, but love was no guarantee that a mortal would not fall from favor. He felt so helpless in this regard. He hoped it would be different after the ceremony.

"Aren't I allowed to be excited about my powers?"

"Yes, your exuberance is inspiring." She still held her fixed gaze, but she did smile.

"You have something else on your mind, then?" he asked, more bravely than he felt.

"After tonight you must not lie with anyone until Witches' Eve. I will consummate your powers, but before the ceremony, before you are brought before the altar, you must not have intercourse with anyone—including me. Do you understand?"

"Yeah, sure. It's like one of those religious things where you have to stay pure until you're initiated—"

"No." She sat up in bed with her back to him, as if she were looking through the bedroom wall and beyond. "It is important that I take you at the right moment, in the right place, at the appropriate time, or else all that we have worked for will be lost."

"Alright. But it will be hard to keep my hands off of you until then," he said, grinning.

"I will not come for you anymore."

"I don't understand—" he began.

"Tonight is the last time we will be together until the Eve. Even if I come to you and beg for you to take me, you must refuse."

"But why would you come for me and have me tell you no? I don't understand. What's it all—"

She placed her fingertips on his mouth, but what hushed him were her eyes. They were red pools, the tinged edges liquid in their movement as they glowed and radiated in a circle as she looked at him.

"Whoever will come in my form will want to rob us of our time. You must refuse, for we cannot take a man against his will. Even if the one who comes in my form threatens you with your very life—you must not succumb. For, if it were me, I would not be here and I would never threaten to hurt you. So, someone else will be here, not I. And only I must take you on the Eve. Do you understand?"

"Someone might try to trick me. No matter what happens I will not have intercourse with anyone until I am brought before the altar on Witches' Eve, and then only by you." He repeated it in a steady voice that was deadly serious.

Her eyes returned to their dark brown richness, and she smiled. As she stroked his face, she added: "Do not be concerned if you are threatened. No one would dare to hurt you, for I would kill them. You are perfectly safe." She lay down in his arms and cuddled into his shoulder. It was exasperating! One moment, more mysterious and spine-tingling than a person could stand, and then she curled up in his arms like a steady girl from school. Questions burned away in his mind. He chose a safe one.

"Why do you talk two different ways? I mean, sometimes you sound like I do and at other times you sound sort of medieval."

She lazily rose to her elbow and played with the curl at his forehead. "That's because I am medieval. I've been around for centuries. We immigrated from Europe. As the years have passed our speech has changed." She opened her hand into the air, and the jar of ointment appeared with a small blinding flash of light. "It is time," she whispered with a gentle, throaty tone. She began the ointment ritual, which would culminate with their final lovemaking session until the ceremony. Jesse hoped that the rest of his questions would be so readily answered, come Witches' Eve.

Essadora screeched as she dissipated the wind storm she had created at Hatisha's house. She found herself hovering over a field in the town of Hoopersville. Her rage consumed her and she emitted lightning bolts from her fingertip as she pointed out the objects she wanted burned or destroyed. The black clouds overhead draped an evil background, and the thunder's booming symphony accompanied her lightning spears to heighten her excitement. Deftly, she flew throughout the orchards and fields, seeking things to destroy the same way she wanted so desperately to destroy Tamara.

"Rain, rain!" she screamed at the bloated clouds. Pointing her hands, she released ten lightning bolts with a deafening explosion that ripped into the night to bring the torrent of water that followed.

Animals fled, trying to avoid Essadora's rage. She glared at a dirt road between the cornfield and a row of trees, and she waved her hand, her look darkly evil. The ground beneath the road began to tremble and it rose up like bread in the oven before the hump thundered along the road as if a gigantic gopher were tunneling under the dirt road, uprooting trees, cracking foundations, and overturning a tractor.

Essadora spread her arms in front of herself, her palms facing outward, her eyes wide with effort as she concentrated on the corn stalks. One by one they slowly plucked themselves from the soil and launched themselves into the air like corks from champagne bottles. The sight caused her to laugh as the launching corn picked up momentum until the entire field was empty.

Next, her look rested upon the barn at the other side of the field. Almost instantly the wood planks pulled themselves from the barn's frame and flew through the air like missiles, landing in neighboring farms. The frame of the barn lifted into the air, twirling around like a top, as it rocketed into the clouds and out of view.

It wasn't enough. Essadora screeched in frustration as she looked around herself. She wasn't getting the satisfaction she craved, the satisfaction she deserved. She needed more sport, and fate was about to provide it.

Charlie Martin couldn't believe what he saw. He stood dumbfounded, his shotgun at his side, watching what appeared to be a woman in flowing robes hovering over his orchard. He was wet from the downpour, but she seemed untouched. He had been drawn from his warm hearth by the eerie lights and the deafening sounds. After tugging on his rain gear, he had armed himself and started out to his fields at a steady clip, but he was soon halted by this strange sight.

Essadora felt his presence. She turned to look at him, her eyes burning red with liquid fire. Her steel-like gaze fixed on his bewildered face as she slowly lowered herself to the ground.

The thunder roared around them as she moved steadily toward him. Her eyes glowing, her mouth twisted up into a cruel smile. He became frightened. Lifting his shotgun was an almost impossible task, as if he were in a dream. He couldn't tear his eyes from hers. He panicked. He couldn't find the trigger—he couldn't find the trigger!

Essadora knew she was flirting with death. But that was part of her game. She loved to terrify them beyond their wit's end, and then . . . She began to soften. Her eyes returned to normal, her silver-brunette hair glistened in the night. She surrounded the man and herself with a transparent barrier that kept out the elements. She dried the man with warm air as the storm raged on outside. She did not stop approaching him until the barrel of his gun rested against her breast.

As she transformed, his terror melted from him, awe filled him as he beheld her beauty. Her soft hands with their long, lavender nails glided gently up her body to the collar of her robes and unfastened them. She let them drop slowly to her ankles, guiding their pace with her fingertips. His eyes followed the robes' descent to the ground, and desire filled him as they retraced their journey. The shotgun fell away as if by itself as the woman opened her arms to Charlie. Her softness filled him as he kissed her wet mouth. An uncontrollable cry welled up inside of him, bringing tears to his eyes.

Never had he felt such desire, such pleasure. He wanted her—no, he needed her. He felt he would die without her in his arms, his lips tasting hers. He felt dizziness spread over him like a warm wave as her tongue probed his mouth. She began disrobing him, her hands moving with experience. They sank to the ground and he let her move on top of him. She stroked him covetously, and he pulled her mouth again to his as she mounted him. Closing his eyes, his desire overtook him.

Never had he experienced such sensations, a bringing of new meaning to his life. His climax rose unalterably and he exploded within her. Instantly, her tongue became bitter in his mouth and she felt wet and clammy upon him. He opened his eyes and began to scream. Her thin, forked tongue snaked in and out of her scaly lips. Green saliva dripped from her mouth as it twisted up into a wicked smile, revealing long, pointed teeth. Her red diamond eyes laughed at him as he tried to push her away.

"Mortal," she began, her voice cackling, "does thee think life's pleasures are yours for the taking? Thee must pay a price.

Give us another kiss." And she sank her lavender talons into the middle of her lizardlike face and ripped it open before his horrified eyes. Charlie screamed and screamed as he pressed himself deeply into the mud, trying to escape the thing she had become. Her whirlwind began again and she disappeared into the clouds, her laughter still haunting the human shell that remained motionless in the mud.

Returning to Brentwood, Essadora realized that she didn't feel as much satisfaction as she thought she should, having put a mortal in his place. She knew to quell her anger she must do something to hurt Tamara, but what? Her thoughts turned to Jesse, and she smiled wickedly. Yes. Wait until Jesse was alone and unaware of the most easily accomplished deceit possible. . . .

Untangling herself from Jesse's arms, Tamara stood beside the bed and cleared her mind. Something was wrong, she could feel it. She watched Jesse sleeping for a few moments before she kissed him good-bye.

She moved through the inner universe and found herself outside of the hotel the strangers were staying in. She had avoided thinking of him all night long as she lay beside Jesse, but now the truth was clear. She wanted this mortal. More than she had ever wanted a mortal in her vast lifetime. She loved Jesse, yes. He would make a fine father for the new race. She loved him with a devotion that sprang from the fact that he was a Maulkian and without that edge she knew she would not have singled him out. She felt guilty finally admitting it to herself.

But this other. This mortal called Richard. He was so much like—like—yes! The Maulkian Tachmann that Hatisha had spoken of at the meeting. That was it. This mortal looked like him—dark hair and eyes, strong of body and limbs, and his scent—she closed her eyes and inhaled deeply.

Richard's eyes bolted open. He lay in his bed searching through the darkness for what had awakened him. He sighed with relief when he found nothing. Wiping the sweat from his face, he sat up, swinging his feet to the floor. His wristwatch told him that it was only an hour since the thunder had awakened him earlier. But the night was quiet now, and it hadn't been thunder that had awakened him this time. He felt as if someone had touched him. A touch that he had felt deeply within. He rose and wandered to the window to see if the clouds had gone and left behind any stars.

Tamara opened her eyes quickly. She had awakened him. She hadn't meant to. Inhaling his nearness had aroused her more deeply than she intended. She had parted her lips and tasted him before she realized what she had done. There he stood in the window, looking upward. She was mesmerized by him. . . . Suddenly, he was looking at her. In only an instant she was gone. He would blink his eyes, trying to focus, and blame it on the night. But once again she had been careless. She chided herself all the way back to Hatisha's house, but she knew what had to be. She must have this mortal if she was ever to be free of him.

The green stalk worked its way out of the soil without difficulty as it stretched itself up to its full height. Its neighbors joining in unison also reached for the clearing skies above, drinking in the nourishing rain and the magic herbs that Hatisha spread throughout the fields as she flew silently overhead. And if a believer had sharp eyes and was very quick, he could catch a glimpse of Hatisha dancing her way through the fields.

Richard brought the car to a stop across the street from Hatisha's house. The clear, sweet smell of morning was quite a contrast to the thunder and lightning of the previous night. The temperature was already into the eighties.

"There it is," said Richard as he swung his arm across the back seat.

"Yep, looks like a house to me," teased Paul, irritating Richard beyond his nature.

"Listen, if you're bored or just not interested in what's going on, then leave! But don't sit here jerkin' me around!"

"Okay, okay, relax! I'm sorry. I admit that I'm a little negative about this whole thing, but I'm only kidding around like I usually do, and it's never bothered you before."

"You're right." Richard sighed. "I'm sorry, Paul. I guess I'm just on edge."

"Listen, if it'll make you feel any better, last night you

could've convinced me of anything, with all that thunder and lightning going on. For the first time in a lotta years I slept with the covers over my head!"

"I know." Richard smiled, remembering the sight. "I didn't sleep well either. I was up and down all night." Richard remembered the woman he had seen briefly through the window. Had she really been there? She was so beautiful.

"What?" Richard realized that Paul had asked him a question.

"I said, what about some breakfast? I'm starving."

"You're always starving. I'm surprised you're as skinny as you are. You eat enough to keep a football team going," Richard said as he started the car.

The old woman watched the car pull away. Her crystal-blue eyes radiated with the image of them as she stirred the yellow batter in the bowl she cradled in the crook of her arm. She chuckled at their conversation about food, and began ladling the batter onto the grill.

Tamara sleepily wandered into the kitchen and gave herself up to the chair facing her mother. She ran her nails through her hair, stretched, yawned and drew her knees to her chest, wrapping her arms around them.

"I believe that we all are doomed," she said groggily. "We are in the thick of it."

The laugh from Hatisha was light and musical. She turned the cakes with a wave of her spoon, and stole a look at Tamara from over her shoulder.

"The mortals call it being in heat," chuckled the old woman.

"Oh mother, please!" Tamara rolled her eyes. "Mortals have such an annoying way of putting things."

"I felt thee tossing all night over that mortal." Hatisha washed her hands at the sink. "Set the table, my dear."

Tamara, leaning on the palm of her right hand for support, crooked the forefinger of her left hand toward the cupboard. Its door opened wide and two plates floated out of the shelf toward the table. Looking away disinterestedly, she spread her fingers wide, and the two plates separated and settled on the table at Hatisha's place and at Tamara's.

"I like the word lust better," continued Tamara as she used

the same methods for the silverware as she had for the dishes. "Why is it that during this time, just before our Holy Day, we have no self-control when it comes to mating? I'm surprised we're not mounting everything in sight!"

Hatisha roared. "Thee does have a way of putting things! This is the only time that we can mate with our men. The power overtakes us, one and all, so that all other things are put aside for the propagation of our species."

"But why now? 'Tis the day before the Eve, why must we run amuck so soon?" Tamara's soft eyes almost seemed pleading.

"My dear, some of us do not feel so put upon," Hatisha gently teased.

"I don't feel put upon. I feel out of control. I have made definite decisions, I wish to stick to them. But how can I if this desire rises for someone other than Jesse?" Tamara brooded.

Hatisha finished putting the food on the table and, settling into her chair, she looked into Tamara's eyes. "What is really troubling thee?"

"Jesse." She drew a deep breath. "I told everyone that he was mine and that no one else could mate with him. But once he becomes as we, he may choose to mate with anyone he pleases. I will have no say. My only hope would lie in his devotion to me, but if he too were caught up in this ancestral need, then his devotion might only win me first place in line!"

The old witch patted her daughter's hand and then, with a wave of her other hand, transported the cakes to the table. They ate in silence and it was several minutes before Hatisha spoke.

"What would thee do if he did choose to be free and mate with your sisters?"

"I don't believe I would like it very much."

"But what would you do?" she asked again, slipping back and forth between old and modern grammar as was her habit.

"I don't know, my mother. I am sure that I would become very angry," Tamara said quietly without looking up from her plate.

"Would thee lose control?"

"Perhaps."

"You must prepare yourself. Your powers are great, you

could destroy us all. Or worse, you could expose us to the outsiders. We would be hounded again until the end of our days.'' Hatisha felt very tired when she spoke those words. ''You did not hurt Jesse too badly the last time he displeased you. Maybe you will be lenient with him again. Your love will be his shield. Prepare yourself for the worst and then you will not act in pain or rage.''

''Yes, 'tis something to think about,'' conceded Tamara as she pushed away her plate. ''I will be gone most of the day. Don't worry about me.'' She kissed Hatisha and dissolved into thin air.

The old woman laid her head back against the chair and toyed with her bent fingers. Her eyes gently radiated with her thoughts and her lips moved silently as if in chant, though she was not. Suddenly, a smile sprang to her face and she rose from her chair.

''A potion!'' she blurted as she danced around her kitchen. ''A love potion. It will be powerful because the lad already loves my girl deeply, but a potion is what we need! I've got to get busy. Got to gather the Kissums and Terramous.'' She clapped her hands and giggled like a young girl. She waved her arms with delight, and the kitchen cabinets' doors opened and closed to her conductorship. ''He will have eyes for no other but my Tamara. And she will bear an heir of pure and noble blood. We will be saved! Must go! Must go!'' She twirled faster and faster, becoming a whirlwind, until the roar of the winds exploded and she was gone.

David held the wet cloth over his nose and mouth as he watched his wife sleep. The black candle had been burning for over twenty minutes on the night table next to Sarinda, its eerie smoke hanging over her like a death cloud. She even looked dead, so still did she lie, except for her quiet, rhythmic breathing. David smiled. The sleep candle would grant him the valuable time that he needed to steal the book from Hatisha's house. He watched his wife's slight figure lying on the bed, and almost snarled out loud. She wasn't much of a witch or a woman or anything. But soon, he would have Tamara and the coven. And he would kill anyone who got in his way—especially that old battle-ax Hatisha. She always seemed to look down on him as if she were somehow better. Well, she wasn't, and soon they would all know it! He slammed the bedroom door behind him as he left, knowing that not even an explosion would rouse Sarinda from her sleep.

"This stuff stinks!" declared Larry as David passed the bathroom. He stopped in the open doorway and watched as Larry soaked in the tub up to his neck in the blue liquid.

"I didn't say that it wouldn't. Remember to wash your hair thoroughly and hold your face under the surface for several seconds. Your clothes will be dry soon, nothing must be overlooked. The slightest untreated skin surface and that old battle-ax will be onto us."

"Hold my face under? What are you trying to do, drown me?"

"I will drown you if you don't stop complaining." David continued on to his study. "Now, hurry up!" he tossed over his shoulder.

David poured himself a drink, half out of celebration, half out of nervousness. The blue liquid that Larry was soaking in would erase any scent or trace of him. The witches could identify the slightest scent of anyone who lived in Brentwood. Like a dog finding his master's scent, they could locate or identify anyone. That, David had discovered, was how they knew when strangers came to town or if anyone in Brentwood was missing. Ordinarily, if someone entered Hatisha's home she could tell the moment that she entered who it had been. Like fingerprints, the residents of Brentwood were categorized in the witches' minds forever. Larry being from Hoopersville would keep Hatisha from knowing exactly who had entered her home if she did catch on. Combined with the liquid, she would not be able to even pick up a scent. No one would know that anything was missing until it was too late.

"Where are my clothes?" asked Larry, dripping all over the wood floors.

"Downstairs in the laundry room. You didn't dry off on any towels, did you?"

"Does it look like it?" Larry snarled, disgusted. He wandered off to find his clothes. David poured another drink. This would be one of the first times that he would test his magic against the witches. He was nervous—hell, he was scared to death! No telling what those crazy bitches would do if they caught him. He swallowed his drink. Soon he would have the book. Soon he would be in control, as long as that asshole Larry didn't screw things up! All he had to do was get the book and get out. The big problem was that soon Larry would turn invisible, both in sight and scent; that was the only way he'd be able to get in and out undetected. That stupid little creep could like his invisibility so much, he might forget all about what he was sent into the house to do. If he wasn't careful, the potion would wear off and he'd be caught literally holding the bag.

"This is wild!"

David caught his breath at the suddenness of the words. Surveying the room, he found no one.

"I could go anywhere, do anything, and no one would ever know it was me!" Larry added, squealing like a child discovering a new toy.

"Just don't let it go to your head, Caylin." David knew he must keep a tight control of the situation or Larry could mess up everything. David himself was trying to deal with the fact that his potion had actually worked!

"Don't worry, this is going to be a piece of cake! When do I go?" His voice moved about the room.

David pretended calm, but his heart hammered away at his chest. He had to stay in control. "Wait a minute. I have to make sure it's all right. The old hag usually goes out for her herbs about now. After her number on the town's corn crop last night, she's probably out there admiring her work." David went to his desk and opened the bottom drawer. Reaching deep in the back, he extracted a small wooden box. Opening it with a silver key from his pocket, David removed a velvet pouch with a matching purple drawstring. He let a quartzlike rock roll into his open palm. The stone, the size of a tennis ball, glittered without direct light and its beauty attracted Larry from across the room.

"What's that?" Larry asked.

"Magic," baited David as he set the stone on the tips of his fingers and held it in front of him. He silently spoke a chant, waving his free hand around it in a slow, circular movement. The center became cloudy and then cleared as it moved toward the outer edges of the stone.

"A crystal ball!" exclaimed Larry as he watched the image of Hatisha's house take form. David smiled with pride; he couldn't help himself, it was an accomplishment for a mortal to have mastered the magic that he had. But he hadn't accomplished it alone; he had help from Phillip Jesoppe, the man who had written the three books he received the night he had met Larry, as well as the four others that were in his desk.

Though the books were ignored by the mainstream authorities on the subject of witchcraft, and despite the fact that not even Jesoppe fully understood what he was writing about—David knew. And he put his knowledge to good use. David had the advantage of living among the witches, watching their ceremonies, how they carried themselves and watching them cast spells. He was like the sorcerer's apprentice without the witches knowing they were being used as role models.

His books told him that crystals were used as a conductor of power. By blessing them and immediately administering the proper chants, a crystal could be used for whatever purposes the chants prepared them for. David had gotten his crystal from a lapidary shop in Butler; studied the chants; and placed the crystal in the cradle of a newborn baby that his wife Sarinda was blessing. The blessing was administered to every citizen born in Brentwood and removed if the mortal moved away. The blessing allowed the mortal to live beyond the average life span. No cancer. No heart attacks. No flu. You lived until your body just gave out, when you just got too tired to go on. As a result, most of the people in Brentwood lived well past one hundred. Once his wife's blessing was over, David had retrieved the stone and recited his chants. The crystal had performed perfectly ever since.

Yes, the books had helped him achieve the impossible, but that was nothing compared to what he would pull off next. Now it was time to get serious.

"Show me," whispered David to the stone, and the image replied by voyaging farther into the house. The stone revealed Hatisha's living room, its hallways and staircases, all came into view on David's command as it headed toward the cellar, the journey's end. Huge, thick candles lit the cellar from heavy golden candelabra. Nine candelabra created an outer circle.

One representing each witch. The inner circle, six feet inside of the outer circle, was painted on the concrete floor with dye from magic herbs. Inside of this ten-foot circle was a five-pointed star whose tips touched the edges of the circle. In the nucleus of the star stood an altar made from the trunk of a twisted tree. Its surface was smooth from ardent polishing, its black wood gleaming in the candlelight as it reached skyward within the limits of the cellar, like two hands joined at the wrists, its open palms facing each other. Its roots formed the steps that reached its bowled branches, whose fingers created a weblike basket from above and behind. And in the crook of the branches, burrowed into the trunk, the altar's flame would be lit on the Eve and the Holy Day.

"Do you see the knot that is in the center of the trunk, just before it splits into the main branches?" David directed his question toward the spot where he had last heard Larry's voice.

"Yeah."

"That's where the book is kept."

"You're sending me in there for a book?" Larry exclaimed in disbelief.

"That book is the key to our triumph over Jesse Trent and any others who try to rule over us." Larry rolled his eyes at David's theatrics as David continued. "Now get your ass over there and get it. I'll be watching your progress through the crystal. And one more thing: don't goof off once you're inside that house. You may be invisible, but you won't be for long. If those witches find you in their house—trying to steal their secrets—they'll castrate you before they'll let you go," David lied, hoping to instill enough fear into Larry to keep him in line but not to change his mind about going at all.

"You don't have to worry about me, I'll be outta that place as soon as possible!"

David heard the tread of Larry's treated sneakers across the floor as he headed out on his mission.

When he was sure that he was alone, David wiped his sweating forehead. His hands were shaking and he poured himself another drink. "Sometimes I amaze even myself!" breathed David with a heaving sigh. It was happening! His wife was immobile due to the magic candle which he himself had made carefully by hand, his potion had turned his lackey into an invisible secret weapon, and soon he would have the book. He set the crystal on the carriage of his typewriter and leaned back in his swivel chair to watch the show unfold.

He began to daydream about how his life would change after he obtained the book. He would read all of its secrets and discover how to become a witch. Once he possessed the power, he would be able to hold his own next to Tamara. She would see that he was the one for her. He would be powerful, powerful and irresistible! He imagined Tamara's renewed interest; how she would see only him. How Jesse Trent would pale by comparison. She would stand before him as she opened her robes, allowing him to slip them from her. He would press his open mouth on her lips; his tongue tasting hers as his hands roamed her magnificent body. . . .

5

LARRY SPRINTED ACROSS the grass and hurdled over a hedge that divided Hatisha's yard from the rest of the neighborhood. He let himself into the house through the side kitchen door. The moment he entered, the hair at the nape of his neck began to tingle. You could feel it the moment that you entered this place, thought Larry to himself. He hurried through the kitchen out to the hall to find the door that led to the cellar. Slowly, he descended the stairs, not because they weren't well lit—on the contrary, the light from the candelabra illuminated everything beautifully—but because the sacredness of the place weighed upon him. He felt the same reaction he felt every time he entered church. He hated going, and only went whenever his parents would drag him along. He wasn't into religion, but this place was a holy place. Maybe not in the same way one thought of God's place of worship, but this was their place. The witches worshipped here.

Of course, everyone knew that witches worshipped the devil and all things evil—so why did he feel as though this was a holy place? He tried to remember everything he had ever heard or read about witches' covens and their ceremonies. Didn't they sacrifice things? People? He shuddered. He found it hard to believe that anyone in Brentwood—even Jesse—would allow such a thing to take place in their town. And wasn't there supposed to be thirteen witches to a coven? What number was Jesse? It would be easy to let his imagination run away with him.

He looked around the cellar once more. The whole place

was like out of a dream. The golden light of the candles awed him as he stood above the star, staring at its perfect lines. The tingling he had felt earlier persisted, and Larry decided that the sooner he had the book and was gone, the better. He hurried up to the altar, and froze.

He had to lean his head back to take in the trunk and the branches. It had not looked so ominous in the crystal. He fixed his look on the tree's trunk where the knot was so that he could muster his courage. It gleamed as the candlelight danced across its black surface.

Larry slowly approached the root stairway. He only had to stand on the second stair to reach the knot. The door opened easily at his tug and the book stood magestically in its chamber. Larry gently grabbed the book with both hands and brought it close to his face to look at it.

David smiled to himself. "We're almost there," he said quietly as he inhaled deeply on his cigarette.

Larry heard a slight sound and he looked over his left shoulder at the stairway, catching his breath. But the stairway leading up to the kitchen was not the source of the movement he had heard. Suddenly, the roots of the tree snaked up and wrapped around Larry's left leg. Startled, Larry stepped back, only to lose his footing and fall backward, causing the book to fly from his grasp and slide across the floor out of reach.

David almost choked on his cigarette. He jumped up from his chair, sending it tumbling away from him.

"Shit! What the hell is going on? I've been in there lots of times and that thing was never alive! You goddamned whores! You did this to me on purpose!" David screamed in a rage.

"Help me!" screamed Larry as another root wound around his leg. He tried crawling away, but the roots only choked tighter. "Help me, Carson!"

David tore apart his desk looking for his books. "You bitches!" he muttered with intense hatred. Finding his books, he tore through them, searching for an answer. "Come on! There has to be something!"

Larry pulled at the constricting roots, trying to free himself. The tree growled with agitation. Its hood of limbs and branches began loosening before Larry's frightened eyes. A giant hand of branches reached out slowly for the book lying near one of the candle holders. It picked up the book delicately with its left arm of limbs as its right branch held the door of the chamber open. It carefully replaced the book and closed the door to its trunk.

"I can't find anything!" cried David as he scanned the book carefully. Grabbing the stone, he spoke into it and his voice carried to Larry as if by a speaker.

"Lie still! You are completely invisible to its senses, but if you struggle it knows you're still there!"

Larry obeyed quickly, his heart continuing its pounding inside his chest. Larry was close to tears as he silently prayed, please—please, let me go!

Slowly, almost uncertainly, the tree eased its grasp. Larry concentrated on the roof of the cellar in a desperate effort not to pull away too soon. The roots rustled as they withdrew back into the bottom of the trunk. They reformed the stairway to the altar, and everything looked the same as before, completely undisturbed.

Larry began to cry with relief. He stayed immobile, lying on his back, staring up into space. David righted his chair in front of his typewriter and collapsed into it. He ran his fingers slowly through his hair and poured himself another drink. He lit a fresh cigarette, and stared into the crystal, watching for any movement. For several minutes nothing moved, and David stubbed out his cigarette and leaned forward in his chair.

"Larry," he said quietly, but there was no response. "Larry, get the book."

"Fuck you," came the soft reply.

"Look kid, I know you got the hell scared out of you, but we've got to get the book."

Larry closed his eyes and laughed softly as the tears ran from the corner of his eyes, past his temples and into his hair. "*We've* got to get the book. That's a good one!" Larry continued in the same soft tone.

"As long as you don't touch the tree you're okay. Just don't touch the tree."

Larry sat up and waited a few moments before trying to get to his feet. He was sure if he made it that far, he'd never be able to stand, but he had to get out of that cellar before the witches caught him. If this tree was only a small sample of what they could do, he was positive he didn't want to see any more of it. Up until now it had been a game to him. Sure he was invisible, and he knew that was impossible, so why was he so surprised to find even deadlier twists to this whole fantasy?

Because, until now, none of this had been real to him. He had been sure that at any minute, some game show host was going to come out of the woodwork with dancing girls and balloons, cameras in tow, and they would all have a good laugh at Larry's expense. But this was no game, and the most chilling part for Larry was how far his hatred for Jesse had taken him. He swayed a bit as he gained his feet, but not enough to keep him from heading for the stairs to the kitchen. The bottom step creaked as his weight went down on it. David realized that Larry was trying to get out of the cellar.

"Larry, don't leave without the book."

"I'm going home and you can go to hell!"

David quickly glanced around himself and then plucked a single hair from his head. He silently chanted over it as he rolled it between his fingers and then gently blew on it before laying it across the image of the door out of the cellar. The handle turned easily in Larry's hand, but the door would not open. He pulled harder, then jerked on it, and finally, out of frustration, he banged on it.

"I won't let you leave without the book."

"Goddamn you, Carson! That tree almost ate me! I'm not going near it again."

"I will not let you leave without the book. We've got this far, where are your guts?"

"I almost threw them up!"

"Get the book."

"No!"

"Then you'll stay there until the witches find you. And I told you what they would do to you."

"I'll tell them about you then. I'll tell them you put a spell on me, and made me steal the book for you. I'll tell them everything!"

"They won't believe you."

"That's what you say." The desperation echoed in Larry's voice as the tears gathered in his eyes. "You just wait—"

"They won't believe you because by then you will have become visible again, my wife will be awake and she will vouch for me, she is one of them and you are the stranger. But the main disadvantage you have is the fact that I am a mere mortal; how can I perform such feats of magic?" David waited for a reply, which did not come. "You cannot win. You will be caught in the cellar. They're monsters, I've seen the horror they can unleash. Go back to the tree. I'll try to open the chamber door from here. Just be careful of the roots."

"All right," conceded Larry as he made his way carefully back to the tree. He stood ready, his heart keeping time like a jackhammer, the sweat beginning to bead again around his eyes and on his forehead.

David heaved a silent sigh of relief and pulled the strand of hair from the crystal, then turned to his books for the proper instructions. To Larry, the wait seemed to be a lifetime. He felt incredibly hot as the sweat stung his eyes. He licked his lips nervously, and the salty taste appealed to his tongue. Monsters, David had said. Larry's imagination could conjure up incredible monsters right at this moment. And why could David do all the things he was doing if he was only human? All Larry knew was that he wanted to get away. This was evil, pure evil. He had had a hard enough time believing in God, but this had convinced him. If there was good, there was evil, and vice versa.

A small creaking alerted his senses to the opening of the chamber door. As soon as it was as wide as it would go, Larry hurried up and jumped, removing the book in midair. But on landing, he came down hard on the roots and the tree reacted instantly in response. The roots waved madly, searching for the thing that had attacked it.

"Get the hell out of there!" shouted David into the crystal. But his words just echoed in the empty cellar. Larry Caylin had needed no words of encouragement about beating a hasty retreat. Relieved, David reversed his incantation and the chamber door shut firmly.

Paul slowly edged through the bookstacks of the library like a crab walking sideways. His eyes peered through the stack shelves, over the tops of the books as he moved to the end of the row. His attention was focused on the elderly librarian standing behind her counter, her own steel-like gaze unfaltering in its perusal of him. Her mouth was drawn down in disapproval and had been ever since the two strangers had arrived. Reaching the end, Paul held onto the shelves and leaned himself sideways out of the stack until he could see the old lady clearly. He then smiled the biggest, toothiest smile he could muster, daring her to return it. The old crone's expression only deepened and her eyebrows knitted together as if she were trying to decide if she should call the sheriff, for surely this young man was not well. Paul's clownish smile ran from his face as he retreated into the depths of the stacks in search of Richard.

"Talk about sticking out like sore thumbs. I bet they don't even have a welcome wagon in this town!" whispered Paul as he reached Richard, who was buried in a book on the town's history.

"One thing's for sure," Richard began as he closed the book, "they haven't incriminated themselves with this town history. It's about the dullest thing I've ever read."

"Maybe there's nothing to tell."

"You're a ray of sunshine, ya know that?" sneered Richard as he put the book back on the shelf.

"Listen, if anybody's a witch in this town, it's got to be the old crone at the front desk. Now she belongs on a broom!" Paul kept looking back over his shoulder; he had the creepy feeling that she was listening.

"Oh, really?" began Richard, somewhat annoyed. He picked out another book from the shelf and shoved it into Paul's face. "How about concentrating on this almanac so you can explain to me why they, unlike the surrounding communities, haven't had any severe crop damage due to weather in the last two hundred years?" Richard smiled as he turned from Paul's startled expression. Startled because he had to do some reading, not because the disclosed statistics intrigued him.

Richard ran his fingertips across the book titles above his head as he moved down the row, searching for something unusual that would relate to their assignment. The sound of small whispering voices came to his ears and he sought out their origin. Two little boys had their heads together in secretive fashion, their eyes occasionally darting around, making sure the coast was clear to continue their exchange of information. With the book stack between the boys and Richard, they were unaware of his presence.

"Is so!" retorted the first child indignantly. His straight, short, red hair and freckles were in contrast with the look of sobriety he wore like a judge's robe.

"Then you think it was one of ours?" asked the dark-haired boy, both excited and questioning at the same time.

"Who else? We're the only ones who's got 'em. My pa thinks it was the mean one." Both the boys shuddered.

"So what are they gonna do with—with—"

"Charlie Martin. 'Member when we hitched with your pa over to Hoopersville to pick up the stud bull?" The dark-haired boy nodded, causing a curl to bounce on his forehead. "Well," continued the redhead as he drew his foot to his lap to tie his shoe, "the guy your pa talked to was Charlie Martin."

"Wow," whispered Willie, his dark head bent in awe of knowing this man.

"I guess they're just gonna leave him in the hospital til his relatives come and get him. My pa said he's got some city nephew in Chicago. If ya ask me, they should ship him off to the funny farm. My pa told our neighbor that Charlie just stares into space and mumbles."

"What's he say?" asked Willie, his big, dark eyes riveted on his red-haired friend.

"He mumbles about thunder and lightning and about," he quickly looked around the children's section of the library where they sat, "the witch and how she turned into a giant lizard."

Richard's heart was racing inside of his throat as he tried to swallow. The witch! He had said it. And she had turned into a giant lizard! And someone had witnessed it!

"Tony, why do ya think she scared him like that?"

"Dunno. Maybe he made her mad or somethin'. All I know is I'm never gonna make any of 'em mad at me."

"Maybe 'cuz it's the Eve," offered Willie.

"Maybe. One thing's for sure, Charlie ain't ever leavin' Butler Memorial 'lessin it's to go weave baskets somewheres quiet." The two boys nodded in unison.

Richard turned on his heel and headed back to find Paul. He found him poring through the card catalog, oblivious to the old crone still boring holes into him with her eyes. Grabbing his arm, Richard whispered to him: "Come on, you won't believe what I just heard. I'll tell you on the way to Butler Memorial Hospital."

"There are no books about witchcraft here," whispered Paul, still rooted firmly in his place. Richard stopped, halted by Paul's unusually serious expression.

"None?"

"No history, no Salem witch hunts, no fantasy books of any kind that would even mention it in passing. Nothing. Nada. Zip." He and Richard looked steadily at each other for several moments, their reporters' instincts in high gear.

"Come on," motioned Richard, and they hurried out to the car.

Larry Caylin tossed back his head, swallowing the Scotch in one motion. He was visible now as he sat in a rocker opposite David, who was poring fanatically through the stolen book. Larry was more of a beer drinker, but at this moment he knew what people meant when they said they needed a good, stiff drink.

Still shaking slightly, he wasn't sure if it was from fright or anger. All Carson had cared about was the book. He had practically ripped it out of Larry's hands the moment he'd returned from that house. Larry thought of the house and the tree that had almost enjoyed him à la carte. He looked at David with narrowed eyes, unconsciously turning his empty glass over and over in his hand. David had said that he hated to see the witches in control, but here he was trying to be one of them. He practiced their magic, knew their secrets, and was even married to one. So how could he say he detested them when he was going out of his way to emulate them?

David was suddenly aware that Larry was staring at him with a look that could not have been mistaken for affection. It was time David soothed some ruffled feathers. His ability to charm was never limited to women. Say the right thing, in the right way, in accordance with the type of personality you were dealing with, and there wasn't anyone who couldn't be handled. He still had plans for Larry Caylin, the party was just beginning, he couldn't let him get away now.

"I've got to tell you, you're one hell of a man," remarked David, placing the book on the desk. The statement caught Larry completely off guard, his own feelings confusing him. David had called him a man. "Yeah, it took guts to do what you pulled off. Don't ever let anyone call you a coward. They don't make 'em like you anymore."

"You didn't give me much choice after you locked the door." Larry spit the words bitterly.

"Maybe so, but don't sell yourself short. A lesser man would have just folded under all that pressure. I couldn't have done a thing if you'd just collapsed into a heap." David rose and refilled Larry's glass and then his own. "No, you're really something. I admire the hell out of you." And he raised his glass in a toastlike gesture before sipping the amber fluid, carefully watching for the sign of surrender from Larry. Several seconds passed. Larry's grip pulsed on his glass. There! The eyes lowered. Doubt set in. He shifted in his seat before drinking to his own salute. David smiled smugly. Larry Caylin would be no trouble in David's experienced hands.

"What if he says he doesn't know you, what then?" whispered Paul to Richard as they entered the hospital.

"The kids said he was really out of it. He probably won't even realize we're there."

"Then if he's out of it, how are we gonna question him, let alone get any coherent answers?"

"I just want to see him for myself."

As they approached the reception desk, Richard went into his "nephew" role.

"Excuse us, miss," said Richard to the woman's back.

"Yes?" she replied, swiveling her chair with a force that betrayed her love of the motion. She increased her smile at the sight of the two men.

"My last name is Martin. My uncle, Charles Martin, was brought in this morning. I flew out the second I heard."

"Oh, yes, Mr. Martin. Just one second and I'll see where we've got him." She smiled brightly at them both before turning back to her card catalog. Paul grinned at her eagerness and cracked his knuckles by interlacing his fingers and turning his palms outward. Richard elbowed him in the side as a warning to behave himself—they were supposed to be concerned about a sick relative.

"Here it is. He's on the third floor."

"Thank you very much," Richard said. Paul lingered behind, grinning at her like a Cheshire cat, causing her to giggle.

"Come, Brother Paul. Didn't the seminary teach you not to dawdle," Richard said from the doorway. The young receptionist quickly returned to her work, embarrassed. Paul turned his head toward Richard with a disgusted look.

"Thanks," he said sarcastically.

"You're welcome."

"Plan 'B'?" asked Paul nonchalantly.

It was hard to believe that the shell that lay in the bed in Charlie Martin's room was ever a productive human being. His complexion was ashen. His eyes were dark and sunken. He lay in the bed as though he were pressing himself back into it. His mouth agape, his lips quivered slightly as he continued staring into the air. They approached the form cautiously and stood staring down at him. Richard leaned close to his face.

"Charlie?" he whispered. The form didn't move.

"I don't think he'll be able to tell us anything," whispered Paul.

"Charlie, what did you see? Charlie, was it a witch?" persisted Richard.

The quivering lips began to build momentum and the balled, almost skeletonlike fists rose slowly off the bed toward Charlie's face. Richard and Paul were transfixed by the sight of his face, stamped with the terror that haunted him. The hands pushed at some invisible object as he slowly shook his head from side to side. His hollow eyes still stared at the unseen thing.

"Charlie, you said it turned into a lizard. What turned into the lizard, Charlie?" Richard was beginning to think that Paul was right, maybe they should leave.

"Witch." The voice was barely audible, but the suddenness of it caused them both to start.

"A witch?" encouraged Richard as he grasped the metal

headboard to lower himself closer to hear.

"Monster," came the voice again.

"The guy's delirious, Rich. There's no way we can verify what he's saying."

"Went to see . . . so much noise." The halting words barely escaped his quivering lips the color of clay. It seemed to take forever for the sentences. "Most beautiful . . . she smiled . . . never known . . . never known."

"Never known what?"

Charlie's chest started heaving and he sucked in his air in little gulps as he tried to go on, his eyes never leaving the thing that was not there.

"Such ecstasy!"

Richard and Paul exchanged puzzled looks. Paul shifted the weight of the camera, rolled his eyes and made mimicky gestures, as though he were berating himself for letting his friend talk him into this.

"I never knew it could be like that." A tear crept out of the hollow and blazed its own trail across the white skin. "I closed my eyes . . . she was gone . . . this . . . this . . . this . . ." Charlie pushed himself deeper still.

"What? What was it, Charlie?" Richard persisted.

Suddenly, the man began wailing as he tried to fight the thing. Richard tried to hold him down to calm him as Paul grabbed Charlie's legs with his free hand.

"Oh, this is good! This is terrific!" Paul whined as he stole a look over his shoulder at the door.

"It's all right, Mr. Martin—Charlie. It's okay now. You're safe. It's not going to hurt you."

Charlie collapsed back into the state of stillness in which they had found him, unmoving save for the slightly quivering lips. They released him, and Richard took his pulse.

"Let's get the hell out of here now, Rich!"

"Alright. I just want to make sure he's okay." Richard watched the form for several seconds before following Paul to the door and down the corridor.

A small glow of white light appeared beside Charlie's bed, spreading into a solid form as Braneesa appeared in his room. Her hands crossed one another as they lay upon her heart. Her closed eyes gave her a serene, peaceful look. Her long black dress swirled about her legs as she moved with dreamlike slowness, unhurried, as if what she must do had to be done with meticulous care. She opened her eyes and looked to the face that stared into oblivion.

Unfolding her arms, she held her hands palms up, out to her sides at shoulder height. Tilting her chin to the ceiling, Braneesa began her chanting. Her arms straightened to their full length as her hands began to glow with a beautiful blue radiance. She turned her palms outward toward Charlie, holding one above his head and the other directed to his feet. As she moved her hands toward one another so that they would meet at the center of his body, Braneesa watched their progress, chanting all the while.

Charlie began to glow the same brilliant blue as the hands passed over him. Once her hands met, they stopped their glowing and Braneesa returned them to their "upon the heart" position. She stood completely immobile as she watched him glowing. Her look was not so much of pity, but that of a superior being who realizes that the lesser cannot take care of himself. Her dark eyes somehow cared for him, and yet hated him for being only mortal.

Pure light rays shot from her eyes, covering his head and following his body length to his feet. That completed, Braneesa returned to her soft glowing light and melted from the room. Her voice came softly to Charlie's ears as he lay in the bed.

"You will sleep now. You had a little too much to drink. You had a reaction to the liquor. You don't know what got into you. You're fine now. You want to go home. Got a farm to look after. Can't be lying around here for no reason, running up medical bills."

Her voice faded from the room, leaving only peaceful silence. The doctors would never be able to explain the phenomenal recovery of Charlie Martin.

Essadora finished braiding the lock of hair at her temple. The rest of her silver-brunette hair hung thick and straight down her back below her shoulders. She always braided the hair at each of her temples because the inch-thick braids gave her something to play with.

"You should be burned at the stake," began Tamara as she appeared and startled Essadora, "but I believe thee would enjoy the pain too much." The icy look masked the hot anger that coursed through her. Essadora recovered quickly from her start and her evil smile slid easily across her lips as she began playing with her braids like a child.

"Oh my sweet sister, what dost bring thee to my humble home?" Her voice dripped with malice, her eyes were afire with hate.

"Why must you play your games so close to the Eve? Sometimes I do believe you want us discovered."

"It would help to know what you are raving about." Essadora settled in a fan-backed wooden chair set with heavy velvet upholstery, her eyes never leaving Tamara.

"Do not toy with me," Tamara began with a controlled voice. She made no effort to hide her contempt. "We all know about the mortal that you scared within an inch of his life, not to mention his sanity. And all for what? Because you were angry at me."

"Don't flatter yourself, Tamara."

"Deny it then!"

"I do."

"Then you are a liar, as well as an idiot."

"Careful where your mouth takes thee."

"No," said Tamara, moving across the room and standing above Essadora, "I am tired of keeping the peace. Tired of your acid tongue, your thoughtless actions that hurt the mortals to provide you with a moment's pleasure."

"And why do you care for the mortals so suddenly? Thee who would not be caught dead with a mortal before thee found Jesse!" Essadora rose from her chair as she began. She didn't like the subservient feeling she got with Tamara standing over her. She went to her fireplace and stroked the cool stone mantel with a perfectly manicured hand.

"I am not the subject of this, you are the one who nearly killed that mortal."

"He was not of Brentwood. The law says no one from our own place. It says nothing about strangers."

"It is almost the Eve! Have you no conception, no grasp of

what would happen if the mortals chose to investigate further?"

"Maybe we should be investigated."

"What?" Tamara was startled almost to the point of rage. "It would mean the end of us!"

"Not necessarily. I have often wondered what it would be like to live among them in their great cities."

"You wouldn't last a week!"

"Oh, no?" questioned Essadora as she turned from the mantel, her interest genuinely piqued. "What makes you so certain?"

"Because you would not be able to control yourself among the mortals. You would be discovered and destroyed! The mortals always destroy what they do not understand."

"Destroyed for displaying my powers?"

"For displaying your stupidity."

"Take care," hissed Essadora, "I am not in the humor to take your words lightly."

"Good," snarled Tamara, "that way you will know exactly what I'm saying and how I feel. It was *stupid* of you to frighten that farmer and leave him as he was without erasing his memory. To let others find him that way so close to the Eve. Mark me, this will not go uncontested. I shall call you before the council at our meeting after the Eve. I will recommend punishment."

"*You* will recommend! I dare say after the Eve, my dear sister, anything you recommend will receive an icy response."

"What do you mean?" Tamara's eyes narrowed.

Essadora twisted up her lips again to the wicked smile. She savored the moment, the confused look fleeting across Tamara's face. "You have claimed the only male within several thousand miles with no intention of sharing him with your sisters. Did you think that no one would object?" She circled Tamara slowly as she warmed to her subject. Tamara stood rigid, her senses ready for the attack about to come. It angered Essadora that Tamara was not even fearful enough to watch her as she moved.

"My sisters understand," asserted Tamara.

"Understand? When none of us has our own mate or hope of children? When each of us would kill for such a chance? We're not about to let you have the only one!"

"You, Essadora, are the only one who would 'kill' for the opportunity, that is why you will be punished for what you did to the farmer. A witch must not disregard life the way you do, for one day she might turn on her own kind and we would be forced to destroy her."

"You will not do anything to me! They now see you as you really are! The blind devotion, the admiration, the respect—you have dashed all of that. Your selfishness has shown through that perfect façade. We will vote to take Jesse from you and we shall all share in his pleasures." Glee danced in Essadora's eyes as she watched Tamara turn slowly to face her, but her smile faded when she beheld Tamara's eyes. The smoldering orbs pierced Essadora to her soul.

"I will kill anyone who takes Jesse from me. My sisters will listen to my reasons and accept them. If Jesse were to roam freely among us he would one day leave, like all the males before him. No, he must mate with only one witch for life. Domesticity will allow healthy children to be born and raised, and soon our race will flourish again. Your way would lead only to pain. Hear me, Essadora, you will not have Jesse!"

"Listen to the empty words! The proud, beautiful Tamara. Ha! You're not worried about anyone taking Jesse from you, you're worried you're not witch enough to keep him!"

Instantly, they both shielded themselves with radiance. It outlined their bodies and glittered like little stars. They circled one another like hungry sharks, almost begging the other to strike first. Fire burned in both their eyes, but it was Essadora who wanted this the most. She needed to get back at Tamara for what she had done at the last meeting. If only she hadn't been caught off guard that way. She had provoked Tamara, perhaps she could turn the knife again.

"If you were half the woman you think you are, you would challenge me without your powers instead of hiding behind them."

"If you want to brawl, then stop bellowing hot air and come on!" hissed Tamara as she let go her shield and stood waiting for Essadora to do the same. Essadora obliged and leapt at Tamara. They tumbled to the floor together, a wild scene of robes, hair and nails. Tamara was the first to rise from the floor. As Essadora rose to meet her, Tamara drew back her fist and cracked her on the jaw with such force that Essadora could only gape with astonishment as she flew backwards across the room. She landed heavily on the fireplace stones, wailing like an injured animal. Slowly, wobbling slightly, she rose. A red line of blood appeared from a cut on her mouth. She spied the fire poker and wrenched it from its berth alongside of the other tools. Holding it in front of herself, she crept toward Tamara.

"This is supposed to be hand-to-hand."

"I don't remember any rules other than no magic, or are you a coward, after all?"

Tamara moved steadily through Essadora's furnishings. A low, gutteral sound came from her opponent as Tamara edged toward a long side table. Essadora charged, swinging the poker forcefully. Tamara ducked the strike and dove toward the table as Essadora swung again, barely missing Tamara's head. The table was lined with plates, glassware and utensils. As Tamara reached for a knife, the poker came down with a resounding crack across her forearm. Shrieking, Tamara backhanded Essadora across the face, forcing her head back with a snap. Her left arm broken, Tamara grabbed a plate and threw it like a discus, striking Essadora in the stomach. The blow caused her to drop the poker, allowing Tamara to seize it from the floor. Immediately, Essadora covered herself with her radiance as Tamara stood above her.

"You treacherous—" Tamara drew back the poker. "It will take more than your magic to beat me!"

"Tamara!" came Hatisha's firm command to halt. Tamara continued to stare with riveting hate at Essadora, who held her arms in front of her to ward off the blow, as if she too doubted her own magic over Tamara's. Hatisha stepped forward, taking the poker, and stood disapprovingly between them.

"Look at the two of you. Behaving like mortals."

"That's all we are, my mother!" Tamara spat the words as she held her broken arm. Her anger was deeper than her mother could remember. "Nothing but glorified magicians pretending to be better than those who were born without this specialty! We rebelled against our own men when they acted like this. We threw them out. But it wasn't really them. It was our entire race. The humans are wild and rebellious, killing one another, not because they came from apes, but because they came from us! It has always been inside of us, we'll never be free of it. Perhaps we should not let it continue. Perhaps no one should mate with Jesse."

"You are hurt and angry, my girl," began Hatisha.

"By all the hell that burns, I am indeed angry! Angry and tired by this soulless creature's plague of evil against me!" Tamara hissed as she glared at Essadora. "But you will plague me no more. Mark me, by all the black magic that exists in this world, if you displease me once more, I shall kill you just for the principle of it." She punctuated her words by pointing a long, red talon at Essadora, then she withdrew her hand and placed it over the swelling on her arm. She glared with fire-red eyes at Essadora as the healing, blue glow emitted from her palm. Once completed, she flexed her wrist and arm to confirm their health. Tamara walked away from the witch on the floor to stand before the fireplace. Turning toward the two, Tamara looked again to Essadora.

"Mark me!" she whispered venomously, the rushing wind swallowing her, exploding, leaving only the silence.

Hatisha used the poker as a cane as she leaned against it, watching Essadora with interest. The beaten woman sat up and began to straighten her wild hair.

"Dear girl, you must have a death wish!" croaked Hatisha. "Why, thee probably would be but a memory now if I had not come to speak with thee about the mortal from Hoopersville." Hatisha settled herself into the fan-backed chair.

"First Braneesa, then Tamara, now you. Why all this fuss over a lowly mortal?" asked Essadora, wiping her mouth indignantly.

"Because you seem to take great pleasure in hurting them. Girl, if it weren't so close to the Eve this might go unreproached, but not this time. The whole episode caused quite an uproar in the neighboring community. Tamara is right—"

"Oh Tamara, Tamara, Tamara! I'm bloody sick to death of her."

"Jealous, you mean."

"And why not? With her around I'll never get my chance to rule the coven." Essadora pouted. The old woman rose from the chair using her new cane, and returned it to the fireplace tool stand.

"I'm afraid, my dear, you will never rule the council regardless of what Tamara does."

"Why do you say that?" asked Essadora, suddenly aware of the tone in the old Maulkian's voice.

"Because, my dear, you do not possess the qualities required to fill that position. The proof lies in your treatment of the mortals. You must be punished." Hatisha reached into her robes and extracted a small clay pot.

Essadora's face grew dark with fear and she began to get up from the floor.

"Do not bother to get up. It will be better for you to remain on the floor. Less distance for you to fall."

"You mean to punish me without benefit of a hearing before the council?" gasped Essadora in disbelief.

"My dear," reproached Hatisha as she dumped the contents of the pot into her hand, "I am the council." The green crystals shimmered in the fading light as Hatisha held them up to chant.

"Oh, please! No, I beg you!" screamed Essadora.

"As the mortal begged you?" Hatisha eyed her curiously before she sprinkled the crystals over Essadora, who began to squirm in agony. Hatisha settled back into the fan chair again.

"Don't worry, my child, I will stay with you until this passes. But you must suffer. Even if you were my own daughter, I would still punish thee. Every witch must be accountable for her actions. We must be better than our bastard offspring or we are finished."

Essadora's skin was on fire. She felt as if an army of ants had invaded her hair and clothing as she tore at her robes. Her head pounded and her ears rang and, try as she might, she could not scream out, for the crystals prevented her from making a sound. She lay on the floor, writhing in pain, under the watchful eye of Hatisha the eldest witch and source of her punishment.

6

PAUL AND RICHARD had sat through dinner without uttering a word. Each was lost in his own thoughts as he tried to sort out his feelings about the day's occurrences. Now Paul sat in front of the television set, not really concerned with the images that flashed before him. He looked over at Richard propped up in bed staring into space, almost as Charlie had done but without the look of horror.

Paul had worried about his friend after the breakup of his relationship with Debra. You'd never pair two people more perfect for one another than those two, yet she and Richard had parted. Richard never would totally explain why. It was hard to imagine that another man had entered the picture. Richard was just too damned right for Debra.

No, whatever had happened it wasn't because of another guy, and Paul knew for sure that it wasn't over another woman. Richard wasn't like Paul. Paul would stray at the slightest provocation. Not that that made him a bad guy, he reasoned, his women always knew the score. No settling down for this kid. Paul had always wondered if the breakup of his own parents was the reason for his hesitation to commit himself. But Richard was different. He really could love, really cared, and he wasn't afraid to let a woman know that he needed her. If only Paul could bring himself to do that.

"I'm going for a walk," Richard said, sighing, as he got off of the bed. Paul was startled.

"Want some company?"

"No. Thanks. I won't be able to sleep until I work off some

of this restlessness. You'd better get some sleep, tomorrow's the Eve. After what I witnessed today, I expect we'll be pretty busy tomorrow night."

"If it will help," offered Paul warmly, "I believe in them too."

"Well, you're trying hard on my account, and I appreciate it. Thanks, Paul." Richard returned Paul's warm smile and headed out the door.

Paul stared at the television, changed the channels, and then turned it and the lights off before jumping into the air, twisting around and landing on his back in the bed.

Richard struck out across the street and headed into the trees beyond the town's buildings. The trees were not as dense as he had first imagined, and they opened out to a cornfield. He walked the outskirts of the corn, his hands in his jeans' front pockets, the thumbs hooked on the pocket rims. He watched the corn glowing softly in the moon's light, its golden color beckoning him to do what he had always done as a child. Reaching up, he snapped an ear from its stalk, tearing away the husk and sinking his strong teeth into the kernels. It was sweet, sweet and delicious.

The woman watched him enter the trees and followed him. He was troubled. Troubled and very lonely. Her dark eyes drank in his image and savored the scene as she followed behind him. His blue cotton shirt outlined his body beautifully, even in the moonlight. He loved this place. The trees, the grass and fields, she could sense it. Why he had never returned from the city sooner made her curious. What was it about those cities that the mortals built that lured men so, but terrified the Maulkians?

Richard stopped suddenly and stared at the corn. It hadn't been there when they had arrived in town. Richard examined the half-eaten ear as his mind raced. He had accepted its presence because it was time for the corn to be tall in the fields, it was time for the harvest. He had walked into the field, eaten the corn, and never even remembered that it had not been there the night before. What else had he missed? What else had he just accepted? And what of the neighboring communities, would they too just accept it as well? A sound from behind caused him to turn quickly. Her words came to him, soft and soothing.

"It is delicious, isn't it? It always is. That's part of the bargain." She gently ran her hand across the stalk's length. "I suppose we should have produced it sooner, but we try to stay out of mortal business unless we're asked. Mortals have a tendency to become helpless if we do everything for them. Truthfully though, I think we just like to show off."

Richard stared at her, half in surprise and half in awe. He had never met a more beautiful woman in all of his life. She smiled sadly as she approached him, stopping only an arm's length away.

"My name is Tamara. I am the witch you seek." Her dark eyes sparkled as she looked up at him, her lips slightly pouting in her sadness. The ear of corn dropped from Richard's hand.

"This is impossible," whispered Richard with a disbelief that caused her to smile. But the smile did not lift her veil of sadness.

"You have spent the last few days trying to convince your friend that we are real, and now that you have your proof, *you* don't believe it."

"We?" The reporter's inquisitive mind taking over. The rush of feelings purging the numbness.

"Yes, my sisters and I. Actually, one of the nine is my mother. The only witch as old as your race."

"But," began Richard, his eyebrows knitting together as if they were trying to bridge some thought, "why are you exposing yourself to me by telling me these things?"

"Oh, it does not matter what I tell you," she turned toward the woods to walk, and Richard followed beside her, "for after I am done I will simply make you forget this entire meeting."

"Then why tell me in the first place?"

"Because I am lonely and wish to share your company. And I sense that you are lonely, too."

They walked the length of the trees, away from the town, and the trees deepened into a thick coppice.

The ax splintered the wood with ease and then repeated the action with precision after Jesse placed another log in its path.

It felt good swinging the ax, working his muscles, the warm night embracing his bare torso before the swing of the ax brought a cool, refreshing breeze. Jesse paused in his work to dump a bucket of water over his head, and he reveled in its freshness. The water cascaded down his body, following his lines like a second skin, with his hands traveling the same route as he wiped the water from him with long, graceful movements. He found himself laughing out loud as he shook his head. He ran his fingers through his hair to slick it back and found himself happy to be alive.

"Thee are magnificent," came a soft, familiar voice from behind. He turned to find Tamara standing by the chopping block, her hand gracefully stroking the long ax handle as it jutted up from the ax, still half-buried in the tree stump.

"Tamara!" cried Jesse as he moved swiftly to her and gathered her up in his arms, twirling her around. She smiled shyly at his robust reception and turned her lips to him for a kiss. He savored the moment, watching her beautiful face, her closed eyes, her pouting, slightly parted lips as he buried the fingers of one hand in her hair. Holding her by the hair, he crushed his mouth upon hers in a wild, passionate kiss. He wanted her to know his need, his passion, how wonderful it could be with him. When he finally released her, her face was a mixture of surprise and desire. It took only a moment for the desire to completely fill her eyes.

"I want you, Jesse," she whispered.

"Do you?" He smiled as his fingers traced her face from her cheeks to her lips, her chin and then down her neck to her robes. Their eyes held each other as she unfastened them, dropping her hands to her side as if she wanted him to continue her lead. He glided the robes from her and let them drop to the ground. His eyes traveled from her face to her breasts as his hands explored her. Jesse's smile seemed more wicked than casual as his hands slid to her buttocks, pulling her to him.

"Do you really want me?" he whispered close to her face, his warm breath caressing her lips.

"Yes, yes!" she whispered urgently as she kissed him, her hands tracing the muscles of his back until they cupped his shoulders. Jesse pulled his mouth away, and his wicked smile returned. His hands slowly traced to the front of her body, up to her breasts where they lingered slightly before moving to the top of her shoulders.

"Prove how much you want me." The steady pressure he exerted on her shoulders caused her to slowly sink to her knees before him. Her eyes looked up at him in confusion. Jesse put his hands on his hips as he smiled down at her. Her eyes lowered to his jeans in understanding and she smiled quickly, her eyes dancing in triumph. Her fingertips skimmed the top of the jeans as she drew her hands to the center and began unfastening them. Her pleasure was short-lived, for Jesse grasped her wrists tightly and pulled her hands away from him. Bending toward her slightly, his voice low and husky, he said:

"You cannot take a man against his will. And I deny you . . . Essadora!"

Her masquerade exposed, Essadora transformed before him, still in his grasp, her rage burning in her eyes.

"How long have you known?"

"From the moment you appeared."

"Liar!" she screeched at him. He jerked her up from her knees, and she fell against him as he held on to her wrists.

"What's the matter? Can't take it when someone gets the best of you? Or can it be that you didn't know that it could be so good with me and now you'll never know what pleasures Tamara enjoys all the time?" Jesse couldn't believe how brave he felt. It was as if someone else had taken over the moment that he recognized the deception. Why couldn't he be this demanding and forceful with Tamara? Could it be that his love for her made him weak?

"Mortal, you shall pay for this insult!"

Jesse shook Essadora with a quick jolt and she fell against him again. This time his voice had a dangerous edge.

"Think carefully before you use your magic against me. Tamara wouldn't be very happy if you damaged me in any way. And besides, Tamara says that I will be as powerful as she is after the ceremony, it wouldn't be wise to make me mad, now would it?"

Essadora drew herself up straight, her anger now controlled. "Release me so I may dress," she demanded flatly.

Jesse obliged, and watched her as she put on her robes. Essadora searched for something to say.

"After you are made into a witch, Tamara cannot keep you to herself. You are allowed to choose one or even all of us to mate with if you like. We will all offer ourselves." Now fully dressed, she slid her hands down his chest and around his waist. "I can pleasure you in ways you never dreamed existed!" She leaned close and her tongue glided across his bottom lip.

"After Tamara, you couldn't possibly interest me," Jesse quipped as he returned to the wood pile and resumed his chores as if nothing had happened and Essadora wasn't there.

"You!" hissed Essadora in a low, gutteral sound that made Jesse look up from his work. "You and Tamara will both pay for your treatment of me. Mark me!"

"See you at the ceremony, Essadora." Jesse smiled as he placed another log on the stump. The sound of the splitting of the log by the ax masked Essadora's winds as she disappeared with a crack of thunder.

Tamara bent under the low branches and into the inner world among the trees of the coppice, quickly followed by Richard. She began unfastening the collar of her outer robe as she turned to him. A second robe was revealed as the first one fell away.

"Allow me." She fluttered the robe once in the air and guided its landing to the leaf-covered ground. The black robe spread wide to allow more than enough room for the two of them to settle on. Tamara sat and arranged her silver inner robe around her, causing it to glitter in the moon's light which peeked at them from an opening in the trees above. Richard sat facing her with a million questions swimming across his face. But what troubled him more was the strange power that drew him to her. Of course she was beautiful, but it was more than that. It was a feeling that came from the depth of his soul to well up in his breast, making him hunger for her. What had Charlie Martin said? That he had never known such ecstasy, and then he had cried. The thought of Charlie Martin suddenly crushed fear upon him. Why had he followed her here, away from everyone, deeper into the woods? She reached for the hand that rested on his knee and cupped it gently with her own.

"Do not fear. I am not the witch who caused the mortal so

much pain. It was another, and she has been punished. The mortal has been taken care of. He is well and will return to his home tomorrow.'' Her touch calmed him and the feelings of desire quickly returned. His eyes lifted from her hand and found that she was looking off in another direction as she continued to stroke his fingers.

''If you're really a witch, then why are you lonely?''

She laughed softly. ''Do you think being a witch gives me a special shield against loneliness?''

''I don't know,'' smiled Richard warmly, ''I've never met a witch before.''

''Must I perform some trite feat to convince you? I'm tired, it has not been an easy day for me. I thought since we were both lonely, that we might help one another.''

''What makes you think I'm lonely?'' asked Richard, caught up in the feeling of her hand moving along and up his arm so slowly that the wait was excruciating.

''You wear yours like I wear mine, unmistakable to those who care for us.'' Her fingers delicately slid across his shoulder to his neck where they rested while her thumb stroked his jaw. ''Why did you and this Debra stop seeing each other? You still love her very much.''

''How did you know about her?'' Richard's heart pounded inside of his chest as her hand started down his throat with the same wandering touch.

''I heard you and your friend talking about her.'' They both watched her hand as it descended his chest. Just as she reached the top of his jeans, she withdrew her hand and returned it to her lap. ''I was the cat that you held so tenderly.'' His head snapped up from her hand and his amazement sang out from his eyes. She leaned close to him as she spoke. ''Ever since I resumed my form, I have wanted you to stroke me as you did when I was the cat. I've wanted your hands caressing me, your mouth wanting mine.''

He needed no other encouragement. Taking her shoulders gently but firmly in his hands, he pulled Tamara to him. Their lips met softly, the passion moving them together tighter as his hands went into her hair and hers sought out the smooth skin under his shirt. As Tamara had hoped, he was masterly. Though consumed by the passion that had driven them together, he knew what a woman wanted. Knew how to feed her fire until it was as consuming for her as it was for him. He made love to her with experience that could only come from diligent practice. But yet, Tamara could sense that this experience was not shared with everyone, rather saved for the times when his heart and soul cared enough to lavish it on the woman he chose.

They lay naked upon her robes, tangled together as if they were never to separate again. Her need rose with his, fueled by the sight of his magnificent body. She clung to his wide shoulders as she arched upward toward him. His powerful arms supported them, lifting her. His hands were everywhere, just as she had longed for. Exploring her, enjoying the softness, the sensations, urging her closer, closer.

Her lips explored him with the same longing, the same desire, the same need. His skin tasted so delicious she wanted to devour him. To consume him totally. Her nails dove through his hair, pulling his face back to her mouth. There it was again, the absolute joy the moment their lips met. Would it ever be this way with Jesse when he was older? Could it be?

He knew. He knew what Charlie had meant by ecstasy. But unlike Charlie, he would know only the pleasure. The comfort. And the ultimate conclusion of their desires. He wanted to love her as she had never been loved before. For her to need him as she had made so many others need her. So that he would be the one she would turn to for her fulfillment. Gone was the loneliness, the sorrow, the *pain* of loving Debra and that love never being enough for her. He had given all that he could—more than any one person deserved, and still it wasn't enough for Debra. Blaming him for every time a man had hurt her, ignored her, used her. All gone. His emotions free of her. He was free to float in the memory of this sensual explosion. But would he forget that, too, when the memory of this night was taken from him?

Jesse woke with a start. He had been tossing and turning with strange images crashing through his dreaming brain. He didn't know what they meant or what had caused them, but they urged him out of bed and into his clothes. He had no idea where he was going as he peddled his bike swiftly through the warm night air, but on he went with determined drive. He jumped off the bike and laid it against a tree before walking into the woods. Where was he going? He had asked himself again and again. He felt angry, hurt, but why? The answer was clear when he ducked under a weeping willow and his eyes beheld a sight which delivered the most agonizing pain to his heart. A pain that surely should have killed him, but it didn't. He lived on to continue experiencing that searing heartache.

"Jesse?" Tamara whispered with astonished horror.

Jesse stood fixed in his tracks, his face expressionless, but his eyes dark with pain. Tamara quickly pulled her first robe over her head and tried to go to him, but he stormed out of the coppice, with Tamara following. Richard started dressing quickly. He didn't know who the young man was, but it didn't take a genius to figure out that he was involved with the witch too. As he began to pull up his jeans, a thought occurred to him. He checked his back pocket and found his pen. One thing Richard had learned early on: a reporter never went anywhere without something to write on. He began writing on his bare leg in his self-styled shorthand.

Jesse stormed through the trees, his fists clenched, longing to strike out at someone.

"Jesse, stop!" called Tamara, but he continued. With his head down, he stormed right into Tamara without realizing she had transported herself in front of him. He leapt back, as if he had been stung, and just stood, his chest heaving with anger, staring at her, on the verge of tears that he would never let fall.

"You must listen to me. I must know why you are here. If Essadora has brought about this meeting—"

"Essadora?" screamed Jesse. "You are off screwing some guy and get caught, and you're ready to blame Essadora!" He laughed a bitter note that tore at Tamara's heart. "Get out of my way before I knock your head off!"

"Yes, strike me, it will calm you, and then we can talk," she said, very matter-of-factly. Her remark angered Jesse further, and he stormed around her. She followed close on his heels.

"You have every right to be angry, Jesse. I want you to strike me." He kept walking, so she decided to try a different tact. "Are you to remain a mortal forever?"

Suddenly, Jesse turned and abruptly backhanded Tamara with his fist. The blow sent her reeling, but she didn't fall. She stood like stone before him, enduring the pain.

"Oh, God!" cried Jesse as he threw his arms around her tightly. "I'm sorry, I'm sorry, please forgive me!"

Gently, she held him, her hand stroking the back of his head as the tears rolled down her face. She made no sound as she cried, and it wasn't until he looked at her that he realized she was. He kissed her eyes tenderly.

"I've never hit a woman before," he whispered painfully. "Only cowards hit women! Please forgive me, Tamara." She turned her face up to his, her eyes closed, her mouth waiting for his kiss. Their tender kiss turned passionate, and soon they were smiling at one another because of their love. Then Tamara remembered Richard.

"Wait here. I must take care of the one you found me with." He held her as she tried to leave.

"Who is he? Why him?" The pain still shone in his eyes.

"Wait, there is much I need to explain, but it must wait for my return. I will be only a moment, my love." She stroked his face lightly as she turned into radiance in his arms and disappeared.

Richard stood in the middle of the coppice, fully dressed, the moonlight accentuating his sleek lines. He was relaxed, as if he knew she would return and had expected him to wait. His dark eyes were filled with understanding. He didn't seem the least surprised at her materializing in front of him, as though it happened to him every day.

"I'm sorry that things worked out the way they did," he said as he reached out and stroked her cheek with the back of his fingers. It was the first time in her life that she was treated as an equal; mortals had always been terrified, hesitant about touching her. It had taken Jesse two years to make the first move, and now somehow, this mortal had made her feel that there was no class distinction, no difference between them. But his tenderness only increased her sadness. Why couldn't he have been the one with Maulkian blood? Why couldn't he have been the one to help her save her race? Tamara had never paid attention to the mortals before, and now she was in love with two. She stepped up to Richard slowly, as if she were memorizing every detail of him. She placed her hand over his heart.

"I shall never forget thee," she said sadly as she looked deeply into his eyes. "I wish thee could say the same thing." She began to chant silently. The radiance covered him, and she continued chanting long after the brilliance disappeared, taking Richard with it.

Jesse ducked into the coppice again and watched Tamara as she completed her magic.

"Will he remember?" he asked tightly.

"No. He's back at the boarding house. He'll only remember a pleasant walk through the moonlight."

"Why, Tamara?" he asked as she picked up her outer robe that still lay on the ground, and shook it out.

"Tomorrow night is the Eve. Our race, the Maulkian race, is required to mate during that time because male Maulkians can only father children on the Eve and the Holy Day. Our people, yours and mine, have labored long over the problems of making the Maulkians fertile all the time, as it is with mortals. But no answer has ever been found. So, the mating drive is very powerful during this time. It is the duty of every Maulkian to bear children. Our long lives mean nothing without heirs to come after us. Unfortunately, we did not foresee the near-destruction of every male witch by enemy and disease, so the act of mating has never reached such significance before now." She paused as she pulled the robe over her head and arranged it so that the outline of silver from the inner robe created a border around the rim of the shimmering black outer robe. Looking up, she turned her face to the moon, as though it were the warmth of the sun. "The need to mate drives us. The need cannot go unanswered, believe me when I tell you I have tried."

"Then why didn't you come to me?" he choked out. He wished he could hide his jealousy, to look as calm and matter-of-fact about it all as she did.

"Because you are about to be introduced to your powers. When I take you at the foot of the altar on the Eve, you will become a Maulkian. Not a mortal witch like the ones before you, but a *Maulkian*. I have created you. You are a true Maulkian by right, and by blood, but only I know the secrets that have brought you, or at least will bring you, to fruition. If I had come and taken you before the time was right, your powers would have been released upon you with such a destructive force that I am not even sure what would happen. If we wait until the Eve, your powers will be introduced to you at a more adaptable pace. That is why I had warned you against having intercourse with anyone."

"And you were right. Essadora tried to deceive me tonight."

"What?" asked Tamara viciously.

"Don't worry, I took care of her." His eyes sparkled at the memory of his game. Tamara's heart sank at the look of satisfaction in his eyes. Would he enjoy the power too much? Would he become as the other males, arrogant and conceited? His look turned sad again. He understood a little better now; the pain was still there, but it didn't hurt as much.

"You're not going to have his baby now, are you?" She encircled his waist with her comforting arms, and smiled at him. His arms instinctively went around her.

"If I ever bear any children, they shall be only yours. If it comforts you to know, I will tell you that I have never been with a male at any other time during the year except just before the Eve. You are the only one to know my love all the time. Together we shall build a new race and you shall be a king." She finished in a whisper, pulling his face closer, seductively licking his lips. His passion seized him. Kissing her hard on the mouth, he tried to open her robes. He wanted to feel her soft skin beneath his hands, but she pulled away, smiling. She took him by the hand and led him out of the coppice. They walked together slowly as they went to find his bike.

"Tamara, I want you desperately, and here you are teasing me!" he groaned.

"I know, I'm sorry, but you do bring out the worst in me." She smiled warmly, but kept walking. As they approached the bike, she turned to him.

"Why did you come to this place tonight?"

"I don't really know. The tingling that I always tell you about"—he looked at her to see if she remembered, and she nodded—"well, it seemed to happen stronger this time. And then when I tried to sleep, I kept seeing you with, with this shadow. The next thing I knew, I had grabbed the bike and headed here."

"Your powers are ready. All the instruction I have given you in the past seems to have helped you to tap into them prematurely. Yes, you will be powerful. You will soon forget me, so much attention will my sisters pay to you, you being the only male."

She was surprised at the suddenness with which he seized her shoulders and turned her to him.

"I will never forget you! And I could never love anyone else ever again!"

"After the Eve you will be able to live for eternity," she said quietly as she stroked his face. "That gives the others a long time in which to change your mind."

"I don't care about the others, let them find someone else to spend their attention on. No one exists for me but you! I only want to make you happy."

She put both hands on his chest and looked deeply into his eyes. "Help me bear the new race. That will make me happy."

Paul was still awake when Richard entered their room. He watched silently as Richard went to the bathroom and turned on the light to get undressed.

"You were gone a long time. I thought I'd have to send out the marines."

"Sorry, I didn't realize." He sleepily pulled his shirt over his head and tossed it on the bed before sitting to remove his shoes. Paul watched him with interest.

"Boy, if takin' a walk is that relaxing, I think I'll give it a try."

Richard stood to unbutton his jeans, throwing a quizzical look at Paul. "What do you mean?"

"What do I mean?" began Paul as he sat on the edge of his bed. "You look so—happy. Like a guy on an island about the second week of his vacation. Really!"

"Oh, come on," smiled Richard lazily. "I'm just a little sleepy. Maybe it's all this country air." He slid down his jeans.

"What in the hell?" Paul exclaimed, pointing to the writing

on Richard's leg.

Looking down, Richard saw that the writing stretched from his knee to his groin. It was his unmistakable shorthand in ink. Stunned and bewildered, Richard sat down on his bed as Paul turned on the lights.

"Jesus! What have you been doing, Rich?"

"I don't know—I don't remember—I went for a walk, that's all." He stared at the writing. How did it get there? Had he written it? He must have, but he couldn't remember!

"Well, what the hell does it say? You're the only one who can read that shit."

Richard looked at the writing for several moments, trying to focus. Why couldn't he remember writing it? He finally turned to the words for his answers.

"I met a witch named Tamara in the woods. I had just realized that the corn was ready for harvest, but it wasn't even in the fields when we arrived in Brentwood. She mentioned that a bargain had been struck between the witches and the townspeople. Their silence for a bountiful harvest. She admitted producing the corn magically. She said there were eight other witches, including her own mother, living in Brentwood. She said that she would erase my memory of the entire meeting with her to preserve her anonymity. She is very beautiful, with dark eyes and long, dark hair. She has this aura that I find irresistible. This powerful attraction reminds me of what Charlie Martin was talking about in the hospital. Tamara told me that another witch had hurt Charlie and had been punished for it. She said he has been healed, we must check the hospital to see if Charlie has been released. And then she admitted to being the cat that had entered our room the first night we were here. We're in a shaded area, a growth of trees so thick it's almost like another world. I've marked the willow tree with an 'X' to help verify this story. I don't think she'll read my mind and discover this because this kid named Jesse found us making love and now she's gone after him. I think she really cares for the kid."

Richard looked up as he finished reading. Paul was astounded, his eyes wide and vivid as he bolted from the bed and danced around the room with glee.

"This is great! Amazing! You old dog! Whoooaaaa! You

made it with a witch? What will your friends say?" he teased as he pinched Richard's cheeks.

"But I don't remember any of it!" protested Richard earnestly.

"Oh! That's great! Don't you see? That proves it! She said that she was going to erase your memory, and she did. You don't remember a thing, but being the brilliant guy you are, you wrote out this 'tell-all' or 'My Night of Sex and Depredation at the Hands of an Occult Queen,' as the smut magazines would entitle it, and now we know everything! Oh, Rich, I could kiss you! Well, why the hell not?" he added, grabbing Richard's face and planting a big kiss alongside his temple.

"Come on, cut it out, God!" Richard couldn't help but grin at Paul's enthusiasm. "How do we know this really happened?"

"Easy! We look for the willow tree; God knows there aren't a lot of trees around this place. And what were the other things? Charlie Martin cured; now, that would take a miracle! And the corn. And then there's that kid, uh—Jesse. We'll check on him, too."

"What if this didn't really happen? What if I made it all up?" Richard asked, agonized.

Paul rushed to Richard; going down on one bare knee, he grabbed Richard's face between the thumb and fingers of one hand.

"Rich, this is me, Paul, your friend, your best buddy. Don't do this to me! My heart can't take it. What was it like—I mean her being a witch 'n all?"

"I told you," began Richard, pulling away, "I don't remember."

"That great, huh?" Paul rose as he spoke, and began scurrying around the room getting dressed.

Richard still sat shirtless on the bed, his pants down around his ankles as he watched Paul racing around, planning the search for the willow.

One thing was for sure, they wouldn't be getting any sleep tonight.

7

THE EVE'S SUN broke brilliantly over the tall, green cornfields. The rain from Thursday night's downpour brought new color and life to Brentwood and the surrounding lands. The grass was long and green as it waved gently with the soft breeze playing through it. The sky had never been more blue. There was a definite joy in the air, as if this Eve would be the best yet. The townspeople stepped a bit more lively, greeted one another a little more quickly, and worked harder while drinking in that dazzlingly fresh air.

The women worked just as hard as their men, but instead of laboring in the fields, they were busy in the house, preparing the feast for the Eve. There would be fresh-baked bread, thick brown gravy, lean roast meat cooked all day in a slow oven, and yes, corn. Sweet, buttered corn with a cool, crisp salad. And after the meal there would be dessert. Pies, cakes, cookies or ice cream would be served up in generous amounts, depending on what was loved by the family serving it.

They would return to their homes with the sunset and prepare to stay inside until Monday morning. Saturday evening was Witches' Eve and Sunday was their holy day, and mortals were not permitted to be outside of their homes during that time. No mortal wanted to be. They didn't know what went on, but whatever it was, it wasn't worth risking the wrath of the witches to know.

One person from Brentwood had already been made an example. For the most part, Tommy Parker hadn't really been a troublemaker. But every once in a while, he'd have too much to drink and would have to be poured into his truck and driven home. He was all alone, having never married, barely scratching out a living from his tiny patch of land, so it wasn't surprising that he was restless.

During the middle of one Witches' Eve, he supposedly tried to find out just what went on at Hatisha's house and was caught by the witches. Only supposedly, because no one actually saw him go to the old house, but he had grumbled earlier that day about having the right to know what was going on. He said the town belonged to the people—not the witches—and they were just lucky they were allowed to stay. And he continued to drink until he was taken home.

After the close of the holy day, Tommy Parker could not be found. Not only had he disappeared, but so had his house and any sign that his farm had ever been there. With such a clear example of the awesome powers possessed by the witches, no one else ever dared challenge them or try to spy upon their ceremony again.

But it was the witches' benevolence when left unmolested that tempered Brentwood's judgment and earned the townspeoples' respect.

Paul and Richard had taken their equipment out from under their bed and secretly loaded it back into the car. Taking what was necessary to record with, they had struck out in search of the willow tree. They headed through the trees and emerged on the outer edge of a cornfield. They decided to follow the line of the trees to where it filled out to a thick area. It took most of the night, but they found the coppice and the willow and the *X* with Richard's initials. Richard had stood transfixed with his hand on the *X*, as if he hoped that his memory would return to him by touching the mark, but he remained just as before, totally blank. They video-taped the entire area before jumping into their car and heading to Butler Memorial Hospital.

They were now parked in the lot near the hospital door. Richard was practically asleep behind the steering wheel, but Paul was wired with excitement. For the first time since Richard had approached him with the assignment, he was intensely interested in being here. Waiting, enjoying the sensations that only happened to him when a story was breaking.

When he and Richard had first met the writer who claimed to know of a coven of *real* witches, Paul had wanted to order a fast white van with padded seats for the old guy. But Richard had been interested, and had encouraged the old boy by asking a million questions. Paul liked horror movies. The gorier, the better. But they were only movies. They didn't happen. This old crazy related unbelievable tales of the supernatural powers that these witches possessed. They did more than just practice the religion of witchcraft—they really could perform feats of magic, cast spells, and best of all, unmolested they could live forever!

Paul thought of how Phillip Jesoppe had become an outcast, searching for the witches and growing more and more crazed by his obsession. He had written many books on the subject, he had claimed, but they had to be ordered through special occult bookstores. He also claimed to have lived with a witch for several years, learning her secrets until she had been hit by a car and killed. He didn't even have her body for proof of her existence because before the police and ambulance could be summoned, she had withered away to ashes.

Paul shifted in his seat as the hospital doors opened to reveal a nurse and a doctor wheeling out a man in a wheelchair. Paul leaned forward and narrowed his eyes. The man in the chair seemed very familiar to him; it was Charlie Martin, looking fit and recovered. Paul grabbed Richard's shoulder, giving it a shake, never taking his eyes from Charlie. Richard sat up without a word, fully awake, taking in the scene that Paul was pointing to.

Charlie rose from the chair, shook hands with the doctor and then put on his hat; he turned to leave. The doctor threw a look of bafflement at Charlie's back as she turned away before shaking her head and returning to the hospital wards.

Richard and Paul bailed out of the car with full gear. Shouldering the camera with ease from years of experience, Paul readied his porta-pack and had his tape rolling as they approached Charlie. He seemed taken aback more by their attention to him, rather than by the equipment or the microphone held before his face.

"Mr. Martin, could we please have a word with you?"

"Why would you fellas want to talk to me?"

"We want to talk with you about why you were in the hospital."

"Uh, look fellas," he began shyly, almost embarrassed, "I don't think a guy tying one on is any reason for you news fellas to bring your cameras out here."

"Mr. Martin, do you remember what happened to you?"

"Course I do. I had a little too much to drink. Started runnin' 'round in the suit God gave me. But that's not worth draggin' you boys out here. I kinda be glad if ya'd jes' forget that. I'm feelin' a mite foolish, if ya know what I mean." He tried to move on, but Richard moved in front of him.

"Mr. Martin," Richard looked deeply at him, trying to instill the seriousness of what he was trying to say, "we saw you after they brought you in. You looked half-dead. You told us that you had seen a monster."

"I know I musta looked pretty bad, I had a reaction to the liquor. I uh . . ." He looked around, then leaned closer, forgetting the camera. "I make up my own stuff; sometimes I get a bad batch." He looked up at the camera, turned a little red and smiled weakly. "But I don't sell it or nothin' illegal like that," he assured his audience.

"You told us about this woman who turned into a lizard. Can you remember anything like that?"

"A lizard? You boys sound like maybe you been into the same hootch as me! Go on, now. Don't know of anybody who wants to waste their time listenin' to drunk talk. They all probably got a farm like me that needs lookin' after." He tried to move around Richard, but he was dealing with a professional when it came to not letting a story walk away.

"Mr. Martin, the doctors who treated you, what do they think of your phenomenal recovery?"

"They was more interested in me gettin' on with my life than you fellas seem to be. I had a little too much to drink. They said I was allergic, had a bad reaction. I know you folks at the news got to find out about all the things that are happenin', but I'd 'preciate it if ya'll just let me get on home. Got better things to do than to be layin' around in some hospital runnin' up medical bills.''

He muttered these last few things as he walked past Richard, who didn't try to stop him this time. Paul lowered his camera as he stepped beside Richard, both staring after the man who had once looked like death.

Each witch lay in her own bed, glowing and shimmering in her veil of radiance. Completely immobile, this was why they needed the protection of the town. Now, in their state of renewal, they were vulnerable. Anyone could attack them, hurt—even kill them while they lay helpless in their beds. They could do nothing. They had to suspend all their magic for these few precious hours before the Eve. This revamping process allowed them the strength and stamina required to carry out their magic throughout the year. The townspeople never knew that they were helpless during this time. Fear and ignorance had always kept them away.

That was the way it had been throughout history, in different towns and different times. As the breeds of man had branched out and traveled to the far corners of the planet, so had the Maulkians. Splintering the race, they had lost touch with many of their own kind. There were probably more Maulkians somewhere, so rumor had it, but the witches were frightened of travel. This new world belonged to mortals, not to them. Mortals' fast trains, planes and cars were too terrifying to explore. With all their great powers, their accumulated knowledge, the witches could not compete with man. They were not sure they wanted to. They had become complacent, resigned to their isolated existence. They had lived throughout the ages, but they had not really grown. If Jesse did not succeed as a witch, or if he alone was not enough to secure the race, then someone would have to take on the journey into the world of man. Perhaps Tamara, the strongest and most experienced, would undertake the challenge. Maybe Jesse, with all his human experience, could journey with her to find more of their kind.

The world of man was indeed a contradiction, and the irony of their situation was not lost on the witches. They had fled one disease only to be consumed by another: man, a flawed, belligerent animal bent on destroying himself and anything that got in his way. Filled with doubts, coarse habits, conflicting emotions and superstitions about the existence of deities that represented right and wrong. Even the name and legendary appearance of the Devil the mortals so feared came from beyond their pathetic culture—came from the monstrous creatures that had destroyed Maulkian centuries before.

The God representing good was a natural emergence of the balance between good and evil. Only the witches knew differently; only they realized there was no higher counsel to prepare to meet. But the mortals needed to believe that there was something more to their existence than just accident of birth. Their belief in right and wrong, Good and Evil, Life ever after, kept the mortals in line. Savagery had not yet made its way through the entire mortal race and the witches wanted to keep it that way. Mortals showed promise. They had gentle ways too. Most of them wanted to live and let live. But it did always seem that those decent mortals were overshadowed by the corrupt, the greedy, the infamous. It was surprising that the world hadn't blown up before now, and everyone knew it wasn't for lack of trying on the mortals' part.

But the witches were becoming no better. They were in despair over what looked like the end of the Maulkian race. They too needed something to believe in. Something that left a mark just as important as the belief in their deities held for the mortals.

Sarinda had not awakened since David first lit his black candle. And now that the Eve was upon her, David had no need for it. He knew that she would lie shimmering like the rest of her sisters until sunset, so he must use his time carefully. Although he was familiar with the Maulkian alphabet, David had trouble deciphering the language of the stolen book. Everything about the witches was actually more complex than he had realized. He needed more time, but he didn't have it.

Larry mumbled something as he turned over on the couch where he had spent the entire night after drinking himself to sleep. David watched him momentarily over the top of the book. He was sure that Larry would remain asleep and out of his hair for quite some time. The kid had really tied one on.

Returning his eyes to the book, he turned the page to discover the last third of the book's pages formed a chamber. The door to the chamber was slightly smaller than the page itself, with a five-pointed star carved into the metal, its points touching the edges of it. The difference between this star and the star in the cellar was this one had diamond tips and a ruby center.

"What's this?" David asked himself out loud as he took his feet off his desk and leaned forward in his chair.

David's voice caused Larry to stir as he rolled back over to face the couch. David set aside the stolen book to consult his own. It didn't take him long to find the passage describing magical locks and secret hiding places. The section informed him that he must place his thumb on the ruby center while placing his ring and forefinger at eleven o'clock and three o'clock respectively. All of this must be done with his right hand, curling the remaining fingers into his palm. The left hand must then be raised over his head toward the East, his thumb and smallest finger touching tips, while he repeated a silent chant of a commanding nature pertaining to the opening of the chamber door. David played with his fingers momentarily before returning to his book to reread the paragraph.

"Yeah, right, Jesoppe. You must be a contortionist." David placed his hands and fingers in the proper positions and concentrated on speaking a commanding chant. He waited several moments more, but nothing happened. He screwed up his face in frustration and tried it again.

Nothing.

"Damn it!" He tossed the book down in disgust. Picking up Jesoppe's book he reread the passage thoroughly, paying special attention to each word to find what he had missed.

"Terrific!" David rose from his desk, leaving the book lying open. There were two things that had caught his eye, the word "witch" and "It is best to know the chant that commanded the chamber's door to shut in the first place." How in the hell could he know what the chant was that first closed the door? And besides that, he wasn't a witch, even though he was trying like hell to become one. He went to the bedroom and stood looking down at Sarinda and her glowing radiance. He remembered the first time they had ever made love together.

David, of course, was well experienced in the art of lovemaking and was all set to completely enslave Sarinda with his "tricks of the trade." But again, the joke was on David. He had not known of the "witches' curse"—that after making love to a witch, only a witch could ever satisfy him. The Brentwood witches erased the memories of the mortals they copulated with; without this reprieve, a man would be condemned to only wanting a witch for the rest of his life.

It went against David's ego to have his passions controlled by Sarinda. The mortal women he had been with since his marriage were solely to reinforce his ability as a lover in his own mind before he returned home to get his "fix" from Sarinda. He thanked his stars that she was a weak witch. Had she been any more powerful, David would have been her slave.

His eyes narrowed and became hard as he watched her. If only he had that ability. He spoke to his sleeping wife. "I will do whatever is necessary to get the power. I don't care what it takes, or what it costs. I want the power and I shall have it!"

He returned to his desk and studied the book again. Maybe he didn't have to be a witch to break this spell; he had pulled off so many other spells and chants, perhaps it was just his ignorance of the chant that had first been used to close the door that thwarted him. He sat thinking for several minutes, then, lifting the book, he turned it over and around in his hands. He knew the answers to all his prayers were contained in this volume. Everything he had worked toward since his accidental discovery of the writings by Phillip Jesoppe when he was attending Butler College. The author's single-minded obsession to prove the existence of the witches had allowed David to command the few powers he now possessed and led him to this book. To become a witch was his destiny. His right. How else could he have managed so much if it were not meant to be?

His thoughts returned to the book. What if they never wanted this book to be opened again? It was never talked of or referred to by the others. He had never known of its contents, only its existence after eavesdropping on a conversation between Tamara and Hatisha with his crystal—a dangerous move considering the witches could have sensed him and discovered his new interest in witchcraft, thus ending his ambitions before he even got started properly. If it hadn't been for the conversation between Tamara and the old witch, he would have never known of its importance or where it was kept. Opening the book again, he placed his fingers on the star in the proper positions and raised his left hand.

"Okay, we'll suppose that they never wanted this chamber opened again, so we state the opposite." Silently, his lips moved as he stared straight ahead. Before he could remove his fingers, the door sprang open to reveal an ancient leather pouch within.

Stunned, David slowly and carefully lifted it out of the book. He had never seen anything as old as this. It had to be several centuries old, perhaps more, and the smell of it was indescribable, a mixture of smoke, dirt, rot and hide. His heart pounded quickly and goose bumps raised on his forearms as though something was trying to tell him that this pouch was very important.

Loosening the string carefully, David worked the mouth of the pouch open bit by bit. Tilting it slowly, he tried pouring the contents into his open palm. At first, nothing moved, but then something fell into his hand. He raised it closer to his face to examine it, but the motion caused it to move around in his hand, so David clutched it delicately to keep it from flying away. Slowly, the fingers opened to reveal a crumbling clump of black ashes. He tested the weight of the pouch he still held in his right palm; it seemed filled completely with this ash. He carefully replaced the ash within the pouch and gently pulled the string that gathered the leather closed.

Holding the pouch to him as if he had discovered the greatest treasure, David again read the book, hoping to make more sense of the passages this time around. Hatisha had definitely not written the script that filled the pages before him. He could read her writing very well, but the longhand before him was very old, and definitely someone else's. It was hard enough to have to decipher the Maulkian language, but to try to read this script was like trying to read a doctor's handwriting.

"Okay, let's just suppose that this is where a witch lives. What do we say, 'Good day, madame, would you just happen to be the witch of the house?' I mean, come on, Rich!" Paul implored as Richard reached for the knocker on Hatisha's door.

"We won't have to say anything like that." He lifted the knocker and banged it several times. "They already know who we are and why we're here. I'm just going to insist they give us an interview straight out. What's the worst they could do to us?"

"Kill us, comes to mind."

"If they wanted to kill us then why didn't they do that before now? Why did Tamara let me go and just erase my memory? They must have some compassion or why would she have been so concerned about my feelings about Debra?"

Richard knocked again.

"Who knows what a broad'll do when she's horny? Why didn't I stay home with Nancy?" Paul turned from the door. "I could be nestled between two huge, beautiful br—uh, Rich, we've got company."

Richard turned around to find several dozen men standing on the street in front of the house and heading up the walk. He and Paul exchanged a wary look as a large man stepped forward. He looked as though he were straight out of a photograph collection of farmers who had spent their lives working the land. His face was weathered, his hands big and rough, his eyes strong with purpose. He paused at the foot of the porch, but his slim frame stood even with Richard's.

"Can I help you boys with anything?"

"No, we were just leaving," volunteered Paul, but Richard's hand on his shoulder kept him from moving.

"We came to see the lady of this house about a private matter." Richard's voice was firm, but pleasant.

"As you can see, the lady isn't home, but I'll be glad to give her any message that you'd care to leave."

"No, thank you. We'll come back later."

"No," said Jonathan Webster firmly as he barred Richard's way, "you'll have to leave your message because you won't be here later to deliver it personally."

"And why is that?" asked Richard, meeting the man's steady gaze. Jonathan looked over his right shoulder as a man stepped out of the crowd and set down two suitcases. The man looked familiar, and Richard and Paul recognized him as Jethro Feeders from the boarding house.

"Because you just checked out." Jonathan's smile was pleasant, but noncommital. "We brought your luggage so there's no need for you boys to go back to your room, you can just head straight out of town. It was nice of you to visit, hope you come back again. Try us in the winter, we have the mildest winters here in Brentwood, I'm sure you'd enjoy them."

Richard and Paul walked past the men and picked up their luggage on the way to their car. Paul whispered to Richard under his breath as they approached the car.

"I was wrong, they do have a welcome wagon. Only this one's called 'The Outta Town On A Rail Service.' "

They piled into the car and slowly pulled through the crowd, and the men watched them drive away. Jonathan motioned a young man from the group, and he loped over to him with an awkward gait.

"Billy, I want you to make sure that they get all the way out of town, you understand me?"

The youth nodded vigorously as he backed away, rubbing his hands on his coveralls as though he were trying to clean them. He let out a practiced yell, and several other young men followed him to his pickup truck and leaped into the cab, the truck bed or anywhere else they could fit as Billy floored the gas pedal. The truck roared after its quarry, smoke billowing out of the silver twin exhaust pipes jutting above the truck's blue cab. The young men whistled and yelled as they beat on the truck's cab as if they were spurring a horse. The truck fish-tailed as its big tires grappled with the road, causing the tailgate to fly open.

Edward Trent stepped up to Jonathan Webster as they both watched the truck screeching out of town. "Do you think she'll approve?"

Jonathan looked over his shoulder at the old house. "She'll approve." He patted Edward on the back. "The boys will keep 'em busy till sundown, after that it's up to the witches."

Edward pressed his lips together as he nodded. The men in the crowd dispersed, and Jonathan looked at the house once more before he too moved along.

• • •

The blue truck skidded to a stop as the road out of town straightened out to a long, narrow strip running off into the setting sun. Billy stepped out of his truck onto the sideboard as he tried to see down the road. The others in the truck looked over the top of the cab, waiting for a verdict.

"Well, whadya'll think, Billy Bob? Did we run 'em outta town or ya suppose we'd better keep on going to make sure?" asked a slim youth who stood on the opposite sideboard from Billy, casually rolling a cigarette.

"I say it's too damned close to sundown to go off chasin' after 'em. Bet they're halfway ta Arizonie by now." The young men on the truck started laughing and howling at the thought of the strangers being run off so easily. "'Sides," continued Billy, "if not, the witches'll take care of 'em come dark anyways."

Had the blue pickup been airborne, the young men would have seen a car headed back to Brentwood using an unconventional route: the path down the middle of a cornfield, running parallel with the highway.

David ran his hands over his sweating face and then wiped them on his pants. Rising from the desk, he made his way to the almost empty liquor bottle and unceremoniously drank straight from it without benefit of a glass. He held up his empty right hand and watched it trembling. His heart and his body seemed to keep time together in an uncontrollable beat. Throwing aside the empty bottle, he combed the cabinet for more Scotch. He whisked off the wrapper, then the lid, and splashed it into a glass as he grabbed a handful of ice from the ice bucket for his drink. The ice felt good to his hands, so he reached back into the bucket with both hands, gathered some water, and rubbed it all over his face.

Burying his face in the bar towel, David began to calm down. How had he come this far? To even consider it? It had all become a mad obsession, yes that was it, an obsession! The power had lured him with its promise of unlimited supremacy. Having known the witches, having tasted the power, however limited, with the chance now within his grasp to fulfill his every ambition—every desire—how could he turn away from it? How could he go back?

He had come so far, learned so much. Hadn't he spent hours combing libraries and bookstores searching for information about witches, only to discover the witches had removed any and all reference to witches or the occult from the local area, causing him to search through book catalogs for what he needed? He had researched diligently until he had discovered Phillip Jesoppe, the answer to his prayers. Though laughed at by practicing mortal witches and witchcraft research experts, David knew that what Jesoppe wrote was the truth. The only problem with Jesoppe was that he didn't fully understand everything about the witches, especially the one he had lived with. Jesoppe had written that sometimes she acted "mad as a hatter," with occasional periods of complete lucidity, but mostly she wandered about like a child. It was in this state that she wandered into traffic and was killed by a car. David tried to combine all that he knew of the Maulkians with what Jesoppe had written, to good advantage mostly, but he didn't know everything, and that exasperated him. Because if what he had deciphered was accurate, he had stumbled onto a secret that made his blood run cold. It seemed that the Maulkians had experimented with the creation of an even more powerful witch! From the writings, he had decided that the tests were completely secret and had been kept from the others by a select few who referred to themselves as the "Elders." At first he had thought only of winning Tamara's love and respect. Then he had thought it within his power to become a "true" witch on this Eve. But now within his reach was the power to become the greatest witch ever to live! But he needed his wife, and he needed Larry. Together, they would help him create the ultimate witch.

"I can't believe you and I ever worked 'Nam together, or that mission in Cuba, for Christ's sake! What the hell makes you so chicken all of a sudden?" whispered Richard as he and Paul crawled through the back yard of Hatisha's house. They took cover against the house as they edged toward the side door.

"*That* was reality, man. *Now* we're dealin' with supernatural shit, and considering that, what you and I know about supernatural shit could fit into a dixie cup, I would tend to say that we are unarmed!'' Paul looked around cautiously as he adjusted the camera to keep it from striking the house accidentally. Richard tried the side door and found it unlocked, but Paul grabbed his arm before he could enter. ''Hey, there's a great movie playing in L.A. if you'd like to change your mind.''

Richard motioned his head toward the inside of the house and entered, leaving Paul where he stood.

''Great, *if* they let us live, it will probably be as frogs!'' Paul followed quietly after Richard. They stood momentarily in the kitchen, trying to decide where to go next. Paul seemed to relax a little after they entered the living room and found it very ordinary-looking. ''What, no black cats or sacrificial altars?'' he joked as he began filming the room.

The room was pleasant and comfortable, with overstuffed couches and chairs that welcomed you with openess and warmth. The floors were covered with beautifully detailed hand-loomed carpets atop hardwood floors that gleamed. Curios of glass and Tiffany adorned the room and one could tell that the mistress of the house had a penchant for glass turtles of any size or description. Richard had felt a strange excitement crawl up his spine the moment he had entered the house. Paul had already been nervous before following Richard, so he was uncertain if Paul had felt the same excitement overtake him.

When they were done exploring the first floor, Paul followed behind Richard as they headed up the stairs. Paul switched hands on the video camera and wiped his palms against his shirt to dry them. This was worse than going through a haunted house on Halloween. At least in a haunted house, you knew something was coming. You expected things to be jumping out at you. Here, there was nothing but deadly quiet. Where staged haunted houses used darkness to pull off their scares, this house was well lit by the setting sun and you didn't know if there was going to be something around the next corner or not.

They each stood on one side of the first door they came to, with Richard nearest the handle so that he could open it as Paul recorded whatever came into view. Richard hesitated for a moment as he reached for the doorknob, remembering Charlie

Martin in the hospital and Charlie Martin being released the very next day. What would they do to them if they were caught? Pushing aside his thoughts, Richard carefully opened the door.

The room before them was completely bare. No carpets, no furniture—nothing. Paul and Richard looked at one another quizzically. The whole situation was a continuing puzzle. There wasn't even any dust, cobwebs—the windows weren't even dirty, but the room was definitely unused. They left the room, careful to be absolutely silent, and continued down the hallway toward the next door.

Again, they took the same positions as before by the door. This time the room wasn't empty. Paul and Richard slipped quietly in and began to explore. The room was completely draped with heavy purple satins. The wooden furnishings were upholstered with stuffed velvets, and on closer inspection, they found the wood was solid cherry. The room appeared to be a sitting room with couches, side tables and overstuffed chairs. Hand-loomed carpets, like the ones in the living room, lay stretched out over the deep purple carpeting on the floor. Paul filmed everything from the authentic antique lamps to the peculiar wall hangings and pictures as Richard examined the draperies. Noticing another door within the room, Paul nodded toward it as Richard looked his way. Again, they carefully opened the door and it noiselessly swung open to reveal the same type of furnishings found in the outer room—but occupying the center of the room was a gigantic four-poster bed with an old woman glowing with radiance within it.

Both men stood frozen in the doorway. Then Paul moved closer in to record the entire scene, giving the bed a wide berth. Richard approached from the opposite side, his look fixed on her, sure that she would awaken at any moment like a vampire from a B-movie. She didn't. Paul signaled that he had covered everything, and he and Richard moved carefully back out into the hallway.

They dared not speak, they simply continued on to the next room and entered just as quietly. The layout was the same as the other room but the colors were black and silver. Instead of hesitating, they headed straight for the bedroom door, Paul recording every detail along the way. The nerve endings in Richard's skin began to dance with excitement as they neared the door. He found that his curiosity had turned from wanting to needing to know the answers—to this house, to Brentwood, to the witch who called herself Tamara.

The doorknob loomed in front of his outstretched hand and his senses were extremely heightened. He felt the muscles in his hand work to grasp and turn the knob. When the door opened, a sharp pang of emotion ripped through Richard as his eyes beheld the woman in the bed. He could not have known her, they had never met before, he was sure of that, he told himself. But from deep within his soul came an ache, a since-forgotten desire. The stunned look on Richard's face stopped Paul cold.

"Is it her?" Paul whispered as he touched Richard's arm gently.

"I don't know—I mean—I don't remember."

"I think you know."

Paul lifted the camera back into position, but in doing so, he disturbed some delicate chimes that hung from the ceiling. The noise startled him and he yanked the camera back, causing him to lose his balance. Richard rushed to help him, but his arm caught the cord that hooked the camera into the battery porta-pak. They both tumbled backward together into a small table, toppling it over with them. The racket was enough to wake the dead.

They both froze, their eyes riveted on the sleeping form. Seconds passed like hours. Heaped over the small, round table, Paul continued to film Tamara, certain that she would rise from her bed and turn them into frogs. When she didn't, the men exchanged looks of confusion, and Richard extricated himself from Paul, the table, and the camera's cord. Paul filmed Richard's progress toward the bed while he too rose from the mess. Kneeling by the bed, Richard watched the shimmering veil of radiance encompassing Tamara. He looked to Paul to be sure Paul had a good filming position, and then he carefully dipped his hand into the sparkling lights. The radiance tickled his senses but didn't stay with him when he removed his hand. He smiled involuntarily, thrilled by the magic before him. Reaching back into the radiance, he softly stroked Tamara's cheek, ready to spring back out of the way if she opened her eyes, but she remained motionless. Paul started to object as Richard began to pick up Tamara in his arms, but then went back to his lens without saying a word. The radiance moved wherever Tamara went.

"I'm going to see if it will surround me as well," whispered Richard as he set Tamara's feet on the floor and wrapped his arms around her, pulling her to him, with her head resting on his shoulder. Slowly, the radiance expanded outward until it included Richard in its veil, the tiny lights twinkling with color and energy. They began to move in a circular motion around the pair as Paul watched through the camera's viewfinder. They picked up more and more speed until the whirl of lights blurred into a mass of twinkling confusion. Richard became dizzy when the lights started to move. They had a hypnotic effect, and he closed his eyes to clear his head. He could feel her so close to him, but the only sound that he heard was the beating of his own heart. She had a beautiful, captivating scent that seemed to surround him. He felt as if he were drifting in a quiet place, dark and welcoming. He lost track of his arms and legs. He couldn't feel Tamara anymore. He was floating, just floating away. It was so peaceful, he never wanted to go back. He wondered idly if dying was somehow like this.

When Larry awoke, David was staring at him from behind his desk. Even if David had been rested and clean-shaven—which he wasn't—he still would have resembled a demon. His eyes bored through Larry fiercely, but he was not actually aware of Larry's awakening; he seemed deeply lost in his thoughts.

"What time is it?" asked Larry hoarsely, wrenching David from his thoughts. Once aware of Larry's return to the land of the living, David transformed into the perfect host.

"It's time we got you something to eat. It's almost sunset. The ceremony of Witches' Eve is not long after that."

The first thing Richard saw when he opened his eyes was the ceiling. But whose ceiling was it? It wasn't familiar to him at all. He heard a small rustling noise, and Paul came into his view.

"Hi there, enjoy your nap?" He grinned above him.

"What?" Richard sat up on his elbows, looking toward the bed where Tamara lay shimmering as before.

"You passed out. Both of you were falling, so I caught the prettiest one and let the floor catch you."

"Thanks."

"Don't mention it. You were only out for a couple of seconds, what happened?"

"She's in suspended animation. I guess maybe they all are, that's why the old lady in the other room is shining too." Richard got up from the floor and rubbed his head and neck. "I felt as though I were drifting off to sleep or some sort of weightlessness; it was irresistible. I bet the reason those men wouldn't let us near the house was because this—hybernation—overtakes the witches and they become helpless."

"But for how long?"

"I don't know, maybe until sunset. Isn't that when they start that ceremony that Jesoppe talked about?" Richard went to the bed and knelt beside Tamara, dipping his hand into the radiance.

"Well, it's almost sunset now, we'd better get the hell outta here." Paul started grabbing the gear.

"I remember last night," Richard said softly as he looked at Tamara. Paul hurried to his side, carrying the equipment. Richard's face was like that of a child making a discovery of some sort.

"Was it hitting your head when you fell that did it?"

"No," Richard whispered with understanding as he dipped his hand into the radiance again. "Somehow, this shimmering light—heals them." He looked to Paul for a reaction.

"Heals them?" Paul skimmed his hand over the surface of the veil. "Are you sure?"

"Right now I'm not too sure about much of anything. But when I went under it was very peaceful and satisfying. I didn't want to come back. This radiance made me feel good. Maybe at this time of year they have to go into this type of hybernation as a way of rejuvenating themselves, like some religions fast before their ceremonies.'' Richard began to stroke Tamara's forehead.

''Since we don't know if or when they'll come out of this—hybernation—let's just move off to a neutral corner somewhere and try to put this thing together. I don't think it's a good idea to hang around here until they do wake up, okay?''

''Yeah, you're right, we should go.'' Richard pulled himself away from the witch and followed his partner out of the old house. He needed time to think, time away from her, out of her influence. It might be more of a curse remembering her than it was to have forgotten.

Sarinda fought the blackness with all her might. She had never had this much trouble coming out of the ''sleep'' before. But this couldn't be the sleep, she had one more day before it would come. This was Friday, yet she felt the sleep all around her. Had she somehow slept through Friday and this was sunset of the Eve? The blackness seemed to turn to a gray haze that was lightening, one veil at a time. She tried to move her limbs but they were leaden. Why? Why was it so difficult to move? Where was David? David could help her.

She tried calling out, but her lips were clamped shut. Through the haze she could make out a shadow. It wavered in its liquid form before her, taking an eternity to settle into a solid border which appeared to be David. He had something over his mouth as he just stared at her with a vicious, satisfied look. Sarinda tried again to lift her arms, but it was impossible. Why was David just sitting there? Why wouldn't he help her? A strange black smoke crept close to her head, and she tried to see it out of the corner of her eye. Then she understood. David was burning a black candle to prevent her from returning from the sleep. This was the sunset of the Eve, that's why she had felt the tingling of the sleep around her. David had kept her in bed throughout Friday until the dawn of the Eve had overtaken her. But he had waited too long to start another candle and she had almost returned from the sleep. Terror crept through her soul as all the possibilities of why David would do such a thing raced through her brain.

Must use my magic, she thought. But the deep blackness

invaded every nerve of her brain as she fought for consciousness. Her eyes pleaded with him to stop, but he only turned away and left her. She was floating off into a black sea of no return, of that she was certain. A single tear escaped her heavy lids, for she understood that David did not intend for her to ever wake again.

8

JESSE INDULGED HIMSELF in a delicious stretch as he awoke. Tamara had been right. The moment the dawn broke on the morning of the Eve, a strange tingling began to overtake his body and a wonderful sensation of well-being and restfulness enveloped him. And just as true, as soon as the sun had set behind his father's farm, the sleep left him and he woke. If the sleep hadn't overtaken him it would have meant that he was not ready to become a witch.

Jesse hadn't worried. There was no doubt; he knew he was ready. Becoming a witch was the most important thing in the world to him next to being with Tamara. He had practiced, studied and endured every trial and ritual that Tamara had tested him with. He was more than ready. Hadn't he followed the images to the coppice to find Tamara?

For a moment his happiness waned as he relived the night before. To see her with someone else, doing with a stranger what they had shared, letting someone else touch her the way he had so many times before—Angry, he clenched his fists, bringing them quickly to his lips, his eyes shut tightly against the evil he was thinking. He heard an ear-splitting sound that whirled him to its source. He blinked his eyes several times, his mouth dropping open with sudden realization. His bedroom window had shattered and fallen into the room. He approached it carefully. Had someone thrown something through it? He looked out into the darkness but saw no one.

• • •

"They've been all over the house."

"The cellar?"

"No, my mother. I think they were more interested in finding us, rather than exploring the house. He remembers, why else would he have returned after all these years? Who was in charge of erasing his family's memory when they moved away?" Tamara furiously paced the room in her blood-red ceremonial robes.

"Sarinda," sighed Hatisha as she sat in a chair near the bay windows of Tamara's room. She straightened the folds in her robes and arranged them about her in an idle pattern.

"The weakest link." Tamara's scowl made her face appear darkly evil. "And he being only a child, she thought it no harm to leave him be! I can just hear her excuses!"

"They are a brave pair," smiled Hatisha with admiration, trying to calm her daughter. "Tis a pity they have no Maulkian blood—such blood would be welcome!"

"Yes, it would indeed." Tamara softened as she ran her fingers through her dark hair, her thoughts with the stranger.

"I think that we should let them view the ceremony since they have worked so hard to discover us."

"You are teasing me?" asked Tamara, turning quickly to her mother, her eyes flashing with alarm.

"I admire their tenacity."

"Others have been just as determined, but we have not encouraged them."

"Ah, but these are believers. A nonbeliever entering the home of a witch is nothing, but to believe in a witch and still enter her place armed only with one's faith, that inspires my imagination!"

"What scheme are you hatching?" Tamara's smile was as wide as her mother's.

"A second ceremony."

"A second?"

"Yes, at the moment that we are honoring our kind, images of us playing out a similar ceremony will be paraded before the two visitors and their cameras."

"Brilliant!" raved Tamara. "They cannot record what can only be seen in their minds, they shall return home empty-handed! Where shall it be?''

''Perhaps it should take place in an area already familiar to our brave adventurers, say the coppice?''

Tamara laughed and took her mother by the hands, pulling her from the chair and dancing her around the room.

''Blessed be! Thou art the greatest to ever live amongst us!''

''Oh, please! You're really dating yourself with that one,'' laughed Hatisha, hugging Tamara. ''Now off with thee. Jesse waits like an impatient bridegroom for his love to claim him. I will ready our theatrical performance for our nosy guests.''

Tamara kissed her mother and then went to her armoire to gather another red robe. Holding it close to her, she spun quickly around and disappeared with the crack of a thunder bolt.

Jesse picked up a large piece of glass and examined it carefully.

''Thee are ready.'' The suddenness of Tamara's voice caused Jesse to drop the glass and quickly straighten to his full height.

''Uh, yes, I'm ready to go.''

''I meant,'' Tamara began as she slowly, sensually moved toward him, indicating the window, ''that thee are ready to become a true Maulkian.''

''You mean, I did that?'' Jesse looked toward the window. Tamara slid her hands up his chest and around his neck. As he turned back to look at her, she kissed him deeply and he crushed her to him in his desire. She slowly licked his mouth as though he were a delicious dessert before burying her face in the front of his throat, kissing down to his collar bone. Jesse closed his eyes in an effort to summon the strength he needed to separate her from him.

''You said none of that before it's time, remember?'' He gave her an amused, yet reproachful look.

''I know,'' she grinned wickedly. ''We'd better hurry before I can no longer be reasoned with!''

Holding out her hand, she pulled the robes out of thin air and held them up to him by the shoulders as the rest dropped to their full length. Jesse took the soft fabric in his hands and he trembled slightly with excitement. Tamara placed her hands on his.

"Come. It is time to meet your destiny."

David pulled the cloth cover from the ceremonial altar he had erected in his own cellar. It consisted of a large, round cement base eight feet across and one foot in height, with a second cement circle on top of the first, but this was only six feet wide and half a foot high. The second slab was concave, with a depth of five inches and a painted star that resembled the one in Hatisha's cellar, its points touching the rim of the smaller circle.

From behind a group of cardboard boxes he brought out another piece of his altar. He placed it on the rim of the outer circle, its semi-circular shape conforming to the ridge of the inner slab, its length covering only a quarter of the outer slab. Painted on this polished concave stonework were the three symbols he had taken from Jesoppe's book.

It had been so easy for him to hide the parts for his altar from Sarinda. Sweet, gullible Sarinda, who never questioned, never entered the cellar, accepting any explanation for why he was spending so much time there. And when he had begun constructing his altar, not even he knew that it was going to be used for much more than originally planned.

He went up the stairs and into the house to look for Larry. He banged on the bathroom door. "What's taking so long?" Larry opened the door, dressed in a red ceremonial robe.

"I still don't understand why I can't at least wear something under this thing."

"It's all part of the fun." David patted Larry's back. "Go down to the cellar and wait while I dress my wife."

"Why are you wearing black and your wife and me are going to be in red?"

"I only have two red ones. You and my wife are participating in the ceremony, so you'll wear those." He watched Larry look down at the robe, spreading it out on the sides to its full length.

"I feel like I'm in a dress."

"Relax," David said with a glint in his eyes, "it's almost over."

Richard looked over at Paul, who was going over his equipment to head off any problems before they arose. They were lying on their stomachs in a cornfield opposite and to the left of Hatisha's house; from this vantage point they could watch the house and see up and down the street. Richard rose to a sitting position and drew up his knee, resting his arm across it.

"I think it's dark enough to sit up now. You about ready?"

"Yeah," answered Paul as he sat up, "ready when you are." He seemed sober and distant, something Richard wasn't used to.

"You alright?"

"Yeah, sure," replied Paul in the same tone, as he scanned the streets through his thirty-five millimeter camera. "You takin' the stills or you wanna work the video?"

"I'll take the stills. I know something's bothering you, what?"

"I'm scared, Rich, more scared than I've ever been in my life." He handed over the camera. "In 'Nam you knew who the enemy was, you knew what the stakes were and what was expected of you. Here we don't know anything. When you think about it, we really don't know what these witches are capable of. Or what they'll do. Or how far they'll go to protect their ceremonies."

"I can't believe they'd hurt us." Richard reached out and plucked the stray grass at the base of the corn stalks. "I'm worried they'll just erase our memories after we go through all this trouble to record this event."

"Frankly, I'd be thrilled if that's all they did." Paul rolled his head around his shoulders, trying to drive out the tension. "But look at what we know: This guy is terrified by something that damn near kills him one day, and the next he's up and around like nothin' happened; you go out for a walk and come back looking all angelic and happy, only to find out that you've been out in the trees making love to a witch who just happened to make you forget the whole thing; this happens to be the same woman I saw our first day here and she disappears into thin air when I call attention to her; we travel through miles of empty fields, only to get up the next morning to full-grown corn ready for harvest; oh, and let us not forget that this same woman claims to have changed herself into a cat to come visit us. Now, this is what we know. Think about it, Rich, think about what we *don't* know. Think about what they might be capable of. These things we've seen aren't simple little parlor tricks; we're talkin' genuine article. It scares the shit outta me to imagine what they could do if they got mad, especially since we're planning to expose them. And considering how hysterical people get when they don't understand things, would you want the world to know you existed?"

"Hey," Richard put a comforting hand on his friend's shoulder, "we're in this together. You've pulled me out of tight places and I've got you out of enough trouble to last a lifetime. It'll be okay, I promise."

"It's outta your hands, Rich."

Their attention snapped to the house across from them as monotone chanting reached their ears and red-robed figures with matching red hoods marched, single file, down the walk and into the street, turning to their right as they proceeded on their journey. Paul snatched up his video camera and went into the trained technician composure that was second nature to him. Though thoroughly engrossed in the scene in front of him, Richard allowed himself a small smile at Paul. The instant he was needed, Paul pulled himself together and was totally professional.

The two men followed the procession along, still hiding in the corn to protect their presence. The chanting sounded low and ominous, the figures shrouded in the blood-red robes brightly lit by the lonely moon as they led their audience away from Hatisha's house.

"We've had quite a turnout," chuckled Hatisha under her breath to Tamara and Jesse. "Something about having a male to initiate, do you suppose?"

"Everyone looks to be here," added Tamara.

"Not quite; Sarinda has yet to arrive. She'll be along, she's never missed a ceremony."

Both Hatisha and Tamara watched Jesse as they spoke, their

eyes darting quickly from his face if he turned, as his own eyes explored the room. He was awe-struck. Never had he quite imagined this, nor could he have, he assured himself. He trembled slightly, his heart pounding out an unfamiliar rhythm, his palms moist. Could the time really be here, had it arrived?

He had thought the last two years had crawled by, but now as he stood before the altar, those years had flown by too quickly. Yes, he wanted to be a witch, a *Maulkian,* more than anything, because it allowed him to be with Tamara. But he also felt as Tamara did: that the power could be put to good use. Sure, he told himself, it would be fun in the beginning, but later on he'd settle down into a routine with Tamara and they would begin their family.

He thought about being able to right wrongs; aid the sick and injured; house the poor; feed the hungry. Tamara had said his powers would be strong. Maybe he could stop wars—eliminate nuclear weapons—free the nations—relieve suffering—raise the dead—become a god! He caught his breath. He shook himself slightly. No wonder Tamara constantly warned him about abusing the power. It wasn't a hard thing to do, even in imagination.

David carried Sarinda to the altar and laid her sleeping form in the bowl area of the smaller circular slab. "She looks like she's dead," Larry said, shuddering.

"She's only sleeping."

"Why'd you knock her out in the first place?"

"You don't think that she would help us, do you?"

David knelt on the large slab with Sarinda between him and the top of the altar. "Here," he pointed, "kneel beside me."

Larry sank to his knees slowly, his look a blend of uncertainty and curiosity. He watched as David extended his arms over his head, palms up in a cupped position, his head tilted back as though he were addressing the ceiling of the cellar. David chanted silently as Larry's eyes looked from David to the ceiling and then to Sarinda as he searched for the slightest indication that something was going to happen.

"What's supposed to happen?" whispered Larry.

"Shhhhhh!" hissed David out of the side of his mouth as he

drew his palms together and down in front of him, forming a triangle. He silently rose, his hands still forming the triangle, his lips still chanting, and moved around the altar in one complete circle.

When he reached Larry, he motioned for him to follow, and Larry rose up and circled the altar behind David, lifting his robes for fear of tripping over them. Once the second circle was completed, David indicated that Larry should wait, and David went to a small table opposite the altar, its contents covered by a blue satin cloth.

Reverently, David lifted the cloth to reveal a glittering chalice and the bag of ashes he had discovered in the book. Carefully, he opened the bag and emptied its contents into the chalice. He brought it to the altar and placed it on the rim of the small slab to his left. He turned and looked at Larry with a sober, serious expression. Dipping into the pocket of his robes, David removed something that he held before Larry in his open palm. It appeared to be a stemless mushroom.

"Eat this."

"What is it?" Larry wrinkled up his nose.

"Quickly, there's no more time!"

Larry picked up the mushroom and swallowed it easily. David moved to Sarinda and disrobed her, placing her hands at her shoulders with her palms up. Larry stared at the scene in disbelief, his eyes questioning David.

"You must have intercourse with her for the ceremony to continue."

"She's your wife!" blurted Larry.

"She's a witch, they do this all the time."

"Well, I'm no witch and I'm not going—not with somebody's—your wife!" Larry caught his breath, he felt strange. A tingling sensation rose from somewhere inside of him and spread like a warm wave to his limbs. "What have you done?" whispered Larry faintly as David held his arm to support him.

"I knew that you might have reservations about this part and that you might not be able to perform the act if you weren't relaxed, so I treated the mushroom with a stimulant." David paused for effect. "Do you want power?"

"Power?" repeated Larry as he realized that he had become

very aroused despite himself.

"She's a witch; if you have intercourse with her, you will share her power. How do you think I learned how to do so many things?" David lied. "How do you think Jesse has been able to do so much?" He opened Larry's robe and removed it without any interference. "You don't have to do anything but enter her. The ceremony will then be complete." David guided Larry over to where Sarinda lay and lowered him to his knees before her.

The red-hooded figures marched around in a circle within the coppice as Richard and Paul video-taped them from the underbrush.

"There's something that's been bothering me," whispered Richard.

"Yeah, what's that?" whispered Paul back.

"We can't see their faces. Maybe we should get closer."

"Hey, why don't we just go up and introduce ourselves, Rich?"

"Paul, you're a shit."

"Yeah. But I'm great at parties."

The mysterious figures stopped moving and turned toward the inside of their circle. The chanting continued as the ominous tones rose and fell in a singsong pattern.

Richard searched each robed figure intently as he tried to search for Tamara. A strange feeling had tugged at his brain for most of the evening and it finally slipped past the veneer that guarded his emotions. When they were done with all of this, could he really expose Tamara to the outside world? Especially when he knew it would bring an end to her life here in Brentwood? Thoughts like these are dangerous, he told himself. He couldn't allow himself to become emotionally involved. Couldn't allow? He almost laughed aloud; he was already involved—emotionally—physically—perhaps even spiritually.

Richard's gaze focused back on the ceremony as he tried not to think about making love with Tamara. Her satin skin; her dark eyes; the taste of her. Now he knew what people meant by finding the missing piece to their puzzle. Tamara was his other half. The part of him he could never fill on his own. Maybe when this whole thing was over—no, he was forgetting Jesse. And Tamara wasn't even human.

Suddenly, a bonfire erupted in the center of the circle and the robed participants took turns throwing things in, causing the flames to change colors and burst into varying shapes and caricatures.

"I wonder if Hollywood's special effects boys know about this group?" Paul said as he watched through the camera lens.

"Maybe they do."

"What?" Paul stole a look at his friend when he realized that Richard sounded serious.

"Think about it for a sec. What if there are more of these witches around, only more integrated into our society?"

"For instance?"

"Athletes who break impossible records; politicians who are constantly re-elected; stars who are multi-talented, singing, dancing, acting—stuff like that. People who are constantly winning awards."

"Like us?" Paul leered at Richard, causing him to cover his mouth to keep from snickering.

"Alright, alright! Maybe it is a little too heavy on the speculation. Maybe these are like the hidden pocket of prehistoric people they recently discovered—wherever it was. But one thing's for damn sure, I'm going to know everything there is to know before I pack up and go home."

Jesse stood before the altar as each of the Maulkian women went to stand in front of her candelabrum that circled the altar in Hatisha's cellar. Hatisha watched everyone take their place, and then she approached Jesse as Tamara kissed him reassuredly.

"Well, young man, what do you think of all this?"

"Hatisha, I—I'm not sure," he smiled shyly as he shook his head, "but I'm glad it's finally going to happen."

"After you and Tamara have spent some time alone together after the ceremony, she will bring you to me and I shall tell you all about the noble race who are your ancestors."

"I'd like that. I want to know everything. When are we going to start?"

"As soon as everyone is here."

"Where is Sarinda?" asked Tamara, becoming annoyed.

"Patience, my love. 'Tis not even past our time yet. I told you she will be here. The only reason everyone else is so ready is our young man here." Hatisha patted Jesse's shoulder.

"Perhaps that mortal husband of hers is causing her trouble." Essadora's voice caused the three of them to turn toward her. She approached them in a slow, sensual glide, her eyes riveted on Jesse's. Tamara's chin lifted slightly at her approach.

"If she were feeling any duress, we would be able to sense it. No, I think David is just delaying her, as usual," affirmed Hatisha, "jealous, no doubt, of our new inductee."

Essadora continued to look at Jesse, totally ignoring Tamara. "I look forward to the completion of this ceremony and the welcoming of you into our race. As well as the exploration of all the options we discussed in our earlier conversation." Essadora smiled wickedly as she turned and went to her place in front of her candelabrum.

"Where is Sarinda?" repeated Tamara, glaring.

Larry didn't know if the strange excitement he felt was from the treated mushroom or the fact that he was now on top of David's wife with his palms placed on hers as David had instructed. He had never been with an older woman before, so he had nothing to compare it with. But one thing was for sure, it was a hell of a lot better than sneaking a feel in the back seat at the drive-in. . .

David stood before the two of them, making the same triangle with his hands and continuing his silent chanting. He began to circle the altar again . . .

"Before our ceremony starts," began Hatisha as she extracted a clay pot from her robes, "I want thee to drink this." She handed the tubelike, slim pot to Jesse and then took Tamara by the arm and led her to her candelabrum. "Do not worry, my child," assured Hatisha at Tamara's questioning look, "it is a potion so that your Jesse will love and want no one else but you. It is my gift so that the two of you can build a life together." Tamara threw her arms about her mother tightly.

"I love thee," she whispered. Hatisha moved to her own candelabrum as she watched Jesse empty the contents of her vial.

David seemed to have taken longer on this trip around the altar, Larry thought, and he wished the whole episode was over, not realizing that it was. David swung the ax with all of his strength, severing Larry's and Sarinda's necks with a single stroke. A human head, severed from its body, could live up to five minutes after the separation; Larry would never know just how long he continued to live on, but the last thing he saw as his head rolled against Sarinda's in the gathering pool of their own blood was David's cruel smile.

The moment the ax severed Sarinda's life force, her candelabrum crashed to the floor of the cellar. Each woman stood rigid as steel, their eyes blinding red orbs. One of their own had just been ripped from them; each knew in her soul of the life now gone. Their minds touched one another in bonding communication as they scanned Brentwood as a single entity.

Gone, too, were the images that had playacted the second ceremony before Richard and Paul in the coppice. Their bewildered expressions were brief as they came to realize the deception.

"Quick," demanded Richard, "play back the video inside the lens, see if we got anything."

Paul shook his head. "Zip."

"Let's get back to the house!" Richard said.

But Paul was already ahead of him.

9

DAVID FELL TO his knees before the altar's pool of blood. He cupped his hands together and scooped up Larry and Sarinda's blood, holding his hands high in offering, causing the blood to run down his arms.

"The blood of witch, the blood of mortal!" David shouted, his voice filling the cellar. Opening his hands, he let the blood empty into the chalice. He then offered it up, as the blood in the pool began to overflow the rim of the altar. He pulled the chalice to his chest and gazed down into the swirling mixture. He hesitated only for a second before drinking the contents completely.

"No!" cried Hatisha as every witch saw David in their mind's eye add the blood to the ashes. "Quickly!" Hatisha yelled as she motioned the others to gather around her.

"What happened!" demanded Jesse again.

"David Carson has murdered Sarinda!" managed a frightened Mazinna.

"He thinks he has found a way to become a witch; instead he has unleashed the very same creature that nearly destroyed our race over a million years ago." Hatisha grabbed Jesse with one hand and Essadora with the other. "Essadora, you will take Jesse to a safe place until we can defeat this creature."

"No!" Tamara was enraged.

"No, I want to stay and help!" added Jesse.

"Listen to me. The male must be protected. Without him our race is lost. Next to Tamara and myself, Essadora is the most powerful witch among us. She will need all her power to protect the male. I will stay here with the rest to buy Tamara some time."

"Time for what?" asked a panicked Braneesa. Tamara felt Jesse's hands on her shoulders as he stood behind her, listening intently as the battle plans were being laid.

"I will not lie about our chances. Other than Tamara and myself, no one here has ever been in a battle before. With this creature, it is second nature to kill. Many of us will die. The only way to win is for the rest of us to try to drain him, to keep him so busy that Tamara can surprise him with fresh strength."

Hatisha grabbed her daughter's hands in her own. "The only way to win this battle is with a cool head and a cold heart. You must take time to collect yourself, to meditate for the marshaling of your powers. You must not think of Jesse or anything else. Your complete concentration must be against the beast."

"But why can't we just escape, and take the male to a new place?" cried Washka fearfully.

"And leave the beast behind to kill off every living thing in his path? He could destroy the entire world if he is allowed to live. No, we must stand and fight; he will seek us out first. For him, no time has passed; he has been restored as if he had never died! Our only hope lies in the fact that he does not know where he is. Only that will buy us the time we need." Hatisha's cold fear was reflected in the faces of the others. Tamara turned slowly to Essadora.

"You must protect him," she said quietly.

"I will," she offered firmly, in a soft respectful way Tamara had never seen before. "I shall protect him for you."

"Protect him for the race, for everyone." Tamara turned to Jesse and kissed him quickly. "Go with Essadora now."

"No," Jesse argued as Essadora took him by the arm. "I want to stay here with you!" Essadora wrapped her arms about him to hold him still as her radiance enveloped the two. Tamara's heart ached at the sight of his disappearing features.

"No time for that now. Go to the inner universe, gather your strength, and only come when you are fully prepared—no matter how badly we might be doing. Your eagerness to help might end it all, now go and prepare," rushed Hatisha as she hugged her daughter tightly before watching her turn to radiance.

"Hold up a sec," managed Paul breathlessly as he and Richard halted their hurried run back to Hatisha's house. They both bent over, their hands on their knees as they tried to catch a breath. The camera hampered Paul's rest.

"Here, I'll take it," offered Richard.

"Thanks." Paul handed it over. "Just for a minute, then I'll be okay."

"I feel like such a jerk!" Richard stormed. He swung the camera strap over his shoulder as he stood, his breathing becoming more regular. "I should have known they wouldn't willingly let us watch the ceremony. We should've known when we couldn't see their faces, or by the fact that they marched right out in front of us. I bet they knew we were there all along!"

"It's not your fault," said Paul as he straightened up. He gestured toward the camera and Richard handed it back.

"She used me." Richard's look was dark.

"She's not the only one in the group, maybe she didn't have any say about it."

"I let myself get emotionally involved. If we don't get a story now, we're going to be laughed out of the office when we get back."

"Hey." Paul touched Richard's shoulder. "I don't know the lady, but what went on between you two doesn't have anything to do with the fact that it's her duty to protect her ceremony and yours to cover it. You're both just lucky that you happened to find some happiness together in between." He dropped his hand and busied himself with preparing his equipment for another run. "Don't tear up the good, Rich, there's not enough to go around in life—take it from me." He began to move off toward Hatisha's house once again. "C'mon. We got a date!"

Encouraged by Paul's enthusiasm, Richard followed him, quickly picking up the pace.

• • •

David screamed in agony as his skin ripped open in every direction. He threw himself about in his pain, knocking over the small table that had once contained the chalice and the bag of ashes. His shrill screams turned deep and animal-like as his height increased to seven feet. Sharp horns pierced his crown on either side of his head and pulled small pieces of skin and hair along with them as they rose to their peak of twelve inches. Claws sprang forth from his fingertips, extending their length by two inches. His jaw dropped down to accommodate his lengthening face as his nose turned snoutlike and flat against it.

Muscles rose under the skin, spreading his shoulders wide with strength, his huge chest burst forth through David's rib cage like a snake shedding its skin. His stomach tightened into rock-hard ripples and his waist declined into a V-shape. His height and width had increased so tremendously that the robes fell from his body in tatters. David's eyes, once blue and seductive, were now black and empty, like the creature's heart.

Dark hair raced out of his skin to cover his hips, and spread thickly over his legs to meet the hooves that now covered both feet. As David disappeared, the beast looked over its shoulder as the skin on his shoulder blades burst open to allow huge wings to push through. The wet wings opened to their full measure, becoming as long as the creature was tall. The sound of hooves echoed in the cellar as the huge creature struggled to its feet, stumbling at first, but quickly gaining its equilibrium. The creature stopped momentarily in front of the altar when the sight of Larry's decapitated body, lying in Sarinda's blood-soaked ashes, drew its attention. A strange sensation at the end of his spine caused the creature to turn to his right, rotating the upper body in an effort to look behind himself. He watched as a long, whiplike tail emerged, completing the creature and restoring him to what he had been over five million years before.

David's mind raged within the creature's. He had no control of its limbs or thoughts or actions. Yet the creature could probe his thoughts and memory at will. The irony of the situation seared him. His whole life had been a cruel joke. The power had seduced him into committing the most horrible crime, and then had left him unrewarded. David now realized if he had only mixed the blood and ashes, the creature would have formed on its own. It was David's ignorance of all the facts surrounding the ashes and his lack of total comprehension of the Maulkian alphabet that had led him to believe he must drink the mixture. The witches hadn't been experimenting with creating a new breed of Maulkian; they had run across this creature whose powers were equal, if not superior, to their own. A lot of good that does me now, thought David angrily to himself.

But not even David realized that the creature he had made was deadlier than its ancestors—because it had retained David's knowledge! Instead of being disoriented and confused as Hatisha had expected, the creature knew where it was and what it was going to do next.

Flapping its now dry wings, the creature rose to hover above the altar in the cellar. It felt as if it had awakened from a deep slumber, and the action of its wings moving helped to drive out the laziness it felt in its limbs. Pleased by the perfect functioning of its body, the creature let go a deep, eerie laugh that was heard as far away as Hatisha's house.

"What the hell was that?" cringed Richard as he and Paul both turned in the direction of the sound.

Purple light shot from the creature's eyes, exploding open the cellar and throwing pieces of it for hundreds of yards. The creature flew out of the cellar into the open air, its laugh sending shivers throughout Brentwood.

"What is it, Rich?" managed Paul, looking up from the ditch they had jumped into at the instant of the explosion.

"Beats the shit outta me," mumbled Richard in astonishment, his mouth open almost to his chest. Paul rolled the video from his prone position while Richard got off several frames of film, his auto-winder working overtime.

"The last time I saw anything that ugly, it had been in my refrigerator for over a month!" Paul joked in an effort to hide his fear.

As if in response to the creature's noisy arrival, thunder crackled through the skies, and black clouds quickly gathered overhead. Six clouds of radiance surrounded the creature as lightning pierced the night in haphazard patterns. Each witch materialized simultaneously with her sisters as the creature rotated in the sky to evaluate its position. Its sinister laugh demonstrated his lack of fear, and Hatisha gave the signal to attack before anyone had time for thought.

Twelve beams assaulted the creature from every angle as the witches directed the palms of their hands at him. He screamed in agony as he plunged to the ground, the beams following his descent.

The two reporters scrambled out of the creature's landing zone. Once on foot, the creature folded its huge wings around it in a protective barrier that the beams could not seem to pierce. It sent lasers shooting forth from its eyes, catching Fleena off-guard and slicing her nearly in two. Washka cried out and went to her aid, forgetting her own vulnerability. The creature quickly took advantage of the error and disintegrated a sobbing Washka as she held Fleena's lifeless body in her arms.

Richard and Paul stared in awe and fear at the scene before them.

"Geez," breathed Richard.

"I take it none of this was supposed to be on the ceremonial agenda, huh, Rich?!"

Hatisha, Braneesa and Corcha all let loose thirty lightning bolts from their fingertips to electrocute the beast as Mazinna, confused and in shock, lowered herself to the ground.

"Check it out!" Paul pointed to Mazinna now on the ground watching the terrible battle continue. The noise of the battle and the thunder could be heard over three counties. Mazinna began backing away from the horrible scene, then turned and broke into a run, trying desperately to flee. The creature's wings partially protected it as it blasted Corcha with its own lightning, neutralizing hers, her radiance protecting her from its effects. The creature sent a fireball spinning after Mazinna, the flames totally engulfing her, melting her where she stood. Its sinister laugh echoed in everyone's ears.

"Things don't look great for the home team!" shouted Paul over the thunder and lightning crashing around them as Richard frantically changed film and tried to watch the battle that raged before him.

The remaining three witches started flying around the

creature in a circle, their speed increasing as the wind they created began to turn into a tornado.

Jesse and Essadora stood on the same hill where he and Tamara had made love on the day of the hockey game. The same place where he had asked for the initiation rite and she had agreed. And here it was, Witches' Eve, the night of the ceremony, but instead of welcoming him into the coven, the witches were fighting for their lives, and he could not help. The entire battle was visible from where they stood due to the magic flying through the air like fireworks. What could he do? He looked to Essadora; her terror was deeply etched into her face. His mind raced with ideas, but he had to have the power before any of them could work.

The witches' tornado plucked the creature from the ground, and it had to use its wings. Hatisha pounded it with lightning bolts, Corcha burned it with lasers from her eyes, as Braneesa hurled fireballs at it from the palms of her hands. The three floated in the eye of their tornado, taking turns blasting the creature as it passed in front of them, carried by the winds. Its wings unable to protect it while in flight, the creature screamed out in agony.

Richard noticed movement to his left and turned to see townspeople fleeing their homes or crouching in the shadows, their eyes wide with fear at the unbelievable drama before them. Instinct took over and he included on his film the reaction displayed on the canvas of their faces. He wondered about what they might be thinking at a time like this. Hell, he was wondering what he was actually thinking about at a time like this. More and more people were now filling the streets or hiding behind structures to watch the impossible scene taking place.

Suddenly, the creature began spinning within its own winds, sending itself crashing through to the calm inner eye, catching the witches off-guard. A startled Braneesa let go her shield and literally caught it in her arms. Quickly, it seized her by the throat, its bruising strength crushing her windpipe and snapping her neck. She hung like a rag doll from its grasp as it moved to ward off Hatisha's magic. The turning to ash of Braneesa in its taloned hand caused it to look at the delicate ashes floating gently to the ground, allowing Hatisha to strike it with an invisible thrust that knocked it to the ground.

Paul bolted, and made it behind a tree to get closer to the creature. He zoomed in as close as he could with the lens, more than adequately recording the Devilin's grotesque features. Richard was beside him in an instant, adding several frames to his ever-decreasing roll of film. Spotting an even better vantage point, Richard motioned to Paul. They waited for the right moment before darting from cover to cover, trying to avoid the wild shots of power deflecting off the combatants' shields. Paul reached safety first, with Richard only seconds behind, when a blast struck at Richard's feet and sent him flying into the cover, Paul, and the camera.

"Remind me to burn my Dungeons and Dragons game when we get home, *if* we get home," breathed Richard incredulously.

"I'll bring the matches," Paul agreed.

The two remaining witches flew at the creature fiercely, palms blasting with searing heat. A huge wing deflected another of Hatisha's beams, sending it streaking over Richard's head, setting fire to the house and fields behind him. The flames engulfed the house, causing the frightened family, who had not dared to leave their home before now, to flee for their lives. The creature sent a fireball after the second witch, and then he shot lightning from his talons toward the running townspeople. The old witch was instantly there to protect the mortals with her shield.

Realizing that the witches' desire to protect the mortals was their weakness, the creature began systematically destroying the town. Hatisha and Corcha split up; Corcha hurried to aid the town, while Hatisha took on the creature alone. She surprised it by disappearing into the inner universe and emerging just behind him. A wave of her hand knocked it off its hooves as her beams seared its flesh.

Get her! Get her! David thought as he fumed impotently. He did not feel the pain the creature felt during the attacks, but that was no consolation. Especially when David stopped to consider that his mind would be trapped within the creature's for the rest of its lifetime and who knew how long that would be? *You moron! Don't let that battle-ax get away with that! Do something, you overgrown reject from a prop shop!*

The creature rolled quickly away from Hatisha's next blasts and took to the air. The beast reviewed David's memory to find out if the witches had any other weaknesses that could be exploited. It was then that the creature discovered that some of the witches were missing.

It climbed higher in the air for a better vantage point. Scanning the town from its aerial perch, he spotted Jesse and Essadora on a nearby hill, standing side by side as they watched the battle. Its maniacal laugh sent the hair rising on the back of Jesse's neck. Essadora took no chances. Quickly, she covered the two of them with her radiance, and teleported them into the inner universe. The beast's lightning bolts missed them only by a split second.

Hatisha knocked the creature from the sky again with another punishing wave of magic. It fell amid a cornfield, and seared it with fire. Hatisha reached inside her robes, bringing out a clay pot. She quickly uncapped it, flying back and forth over the beast as she spread the twinkling powder into the field. The creature gained its footing and prepared to blast Hatisha from the air, when suddenly, the stalks of corn around it came alive!

They wrapped themselves about its legs, arms, wings and neck. The beast bellowed in confusion as the stalks continued to hold it down, their roots entwining constrictively among themselves to form a stronger bond. Light blazed from its eyes at the stalks, leaving them in a black, smoldering heap.

Hatisha dipped into her pocket for another clay pot and flew toward the creature again. Catching her approach, the Devilin immediately swung its lasers around and poured its power at Hatisha, causing her to drop the pot in order to protect herself. She had to disappear into the inner universe to avoid what she knew would occur once her magic crystals hit the ground.

The area strewn with crystals began to tremble and groan before exploding upward: dirt, grass, weeds and debris scattering for several feet. The reporters automatically covered themselves.

"Déjà vu, 'Nam all over again!"

"Not quite," pointed Richard.

They both focussed on the swelling earth where the crystals had landed. One by one, large, fat earthworms began wriggling through the surface dirt, growing larger each second.

Hatisha reappeared and hurriedly sprinkled new crystals over the worms as the Devilin freed himself from the last of his bonds. The new crystals sent the worms back to the dark damp earth below.

Corcha had managed to extinguish the fires in the houses and fields, only to have the creature set more as soon as it could protect itself with its huge wings. The townspeople now fled their homes in droves. Never had an Eve brought terror. Never had their homes or lives been in danger.

The spilling of the townspeople into the streets only added to the witches' burden as they tried to protect them from the creature. Finally, out of frustration, Hatisha left Corcha to engage the beast while she worked her magic to completely transport all the townspeople to Hoopersville and safety.

Paul and Richard relocated to the opposite side of the street alongside a house for more protection and to keep Hatisha from spotting them and sending them away too. They were sure that—unless she saw them—she would be too occupied to worry about them, and they had no intention of leaving—not yet. Richard was kept busy reloading his camera as he quickly went through every roll of film he carried.

Hatisha and Corcha hovered together, signaling one another with quick, precise movements as they readied their next attack. Muscles ached, tiredness weighed their bodies down, but none of this showed in their attack. Hatisha became a furiously spinning top as she buzz-sawed through the air at the beast, causing it to take to flight in an effort to avoid her impact. Corcha plummeted from above like a hawk, seizing its wings from behind. The creature thrashed about wildly, sending them spiraling to the ground together, the Devilin on top of Corcha, his back to her as his body lay vulnerable to Hatisha's magic. The Devilin's roar of panic and alarm was not unfounded as Corcha struggled with all the might of her magic to hold it down while Hatisha flew in for the kill.

The beast met Hatisha's blast of power with its own. The creature's arms were free, and it reached over its shoulders, managing to grasp Corcha's wrists. Though she was protected by her radiance, the creature sent its own magic through its grip, causing Corcha's shield to glow red instead of green.

Hatisha and the creature exchanged fire and lightning, but the beast refused to relinquish its hold on Corcha. The heat of its magic began penetrating her shield and she cried out to Hatisha.

"What shall I do?"

The panic in her eyes cut to Hatisha's soul. The old witch flew behind the pair and landed near their heads. The beast tilted its head, trying to blast Hatisha, but unable to reach her. Pointing, she concentrated all of her powers on the wrists of the creature. It screamed again and again, but it would not let go of Corcha.

"Please, help me!" screamed Corcha as the intense heat of the beast's magic combined with her shield to vanquish her own magic. Instantly, it leaped to its cloven hooves, pulling Corcha with it. It held her by the shoulders, using her as a shield against Hatisha.

"W-it-ch!" breathed the creature in a deep, raspy voice. Hatisha stood before it, her radiance glittering around her protectively. "I shall trade you the life of this one for your own." It smiled as it dug its talons into Corcha's shoulders. She cried silently, trying not to look at the eldest Maulkian, believing that she had failed.

"What's to prevent you from killing her after you have dispensed with me? Your trade is unfair."

"You are the strongest one here. Only you could truly challenge me. Let me go in peace to live somewhere else and I shall spare both of your lives." His hand moved around Corcha's throat as he released her shoulders.

"I could not allow you to roam freely among the mortals. They are defenseless."

"If they pleased me they would have no fear of me."

"You would tire of them and kill them and then you'd be all alone, living on the hull of an empty planet."

"It would not be necessary to kill all of them, just the ones who would do me harm." The creature played with Corcha's hair. "And after a while, there would be others of my kind to keep me company."

"But they would be different—not like what you know. It has been this way for us. Breeding with mortals never gave us others truly of our kind."

"This is what I think of your answer!" raged the beast as it tore off Corcha's head and cast her body to the ground. Instantly, Hatisha blasted it full force with her power, the blow knocking it over a hundred feet away.

"Essadora!" pleaded Jesse, "you must initiate me—there are only three of you left! If he can defeat Hatisha, there will only be two."

"I gave my promise. Only Tamara can take—"

"If this creature can destroy all of your sisters, how can you expect to defend me by yourself?"

Essadora's grave look slowly left Jesse's eyes. She had transported them to the roof of a house, and she now turned to view the battle below. Jesse moved behind her and put his hands on her shoulders as he leaned close to whisper in her ear.

"If you keep your promise," he said urgently, "it could mean the end of us all."

The beast seemed to be defeating the entire coven, and now it was Hatisha's turn. A feeling of euphoria lifted David's spirits at the thought that the bitch was finally getting what was coming to her! Hatisha's revelation about mortal man's beginnings started sinking in but David was still having a hard time trying to digest it. If witches had interbred with mortals, why did the witches still treat them like a disease? Why hadn't they raised them properly and taught them about their heritage? Questions. Questions that would never be answered. Questions that would forever burn. Questions. David watched the creature closing in on Hatisha. *You bitch,* he thought, *if you had only answered my questions.*

Suddenly, Hatisha's attack against the creature ceased. The beast carefully peered around its wings, ready to protect itself once again if Hatisha was changing her strategy. Hatisha stood very still, her hands forming a triangle, her lips moving in silent chant. Though her look was straight ahead at the creature, it was as if she did not see it.

It made a move at her, sure that she would break into

another attack, but she did not move, nor did she cease her chanting. The beast reviewed David's mind, searching for what trick she might be using, its tail swishing menacingly when it could not find the answer it wanted. Steadily, it moved toward her, its huge wing wrapped to the front protectively. Her chanting stopped, and the creature froze in its tracks, waiting for her attack. Her color changed to a solid gray, her eyes becoming empty hollows. The creature became annoyed at this new development and angrily swung a vicious claw at her face. The sound of its talons hitting the ash was similar to kicking a pile of leaves in autumn. Her ashes swirled up, carried by the draft of its swing.

The two young men lowered their cameras as they silently mourned the death of the old witch. Richard had never met her but something told him he would have liked her very much and his heart tugged a little when he realized that now he never would.

"What now?" Hopelessness filled Paul's voice. Richard only shrugged.

The beast bellowed indignantly at the realization that it had been robbed of its kill. It burst through the statue of ash, scattering it about the landscape. Its massive chest heaved with anger.

Throwing its wings back, the Devilin let go a wild cry of doom. It had defeated the coven and now it would destroy everyone.

A devastating blow suddenly felled the creature. Tamara strode toward the beast in a determined, unhurried glide. A smile spread across Richard's face at the sight of her and his affection was plain in his eyes when Paul stole a glance in his direction.

The creature tried to push itself off the ground, but collapsed back into the dirt. It shook its huge head, trying for clear thought. It felt its body rise from the ground, but knew it was not of its own power. The beast turned a sore neck to look over its shoulder at the source of the magic. The dark eyes the beast saw burned with military efficiency, the face unlined by expression. She held her hands up before her, her gaze never leaving the creature, and motioned with her hands as if she were spinning a top. Immediately, the beast spun head over heels in the air before her. Finding it was unable to halt its turning, its voice boomed out in surprise. A snap of Tamara's fingers brought the creature crashing to the ground, then she began the cycle again.

She opened her hand to reveal electrical charges that danced around her palm. They took the shape of several electrical spiders, and she cast them upon the beast on its final fall to the ground. The tiny spiders stung it everywhere as it clawed at them, trying to remove them. But it only succeeded in slashing itself, its blood trickling through the deep furrows now in its skin.

Power shot from the creature's eyes as it tried to divert Tamara's magic. She easily deflected its beams with one hand as she froze it solid with the other.

David's mind screamed at the creature's, reminding it of the male named Jesse. This was her weakness. With renewed strength, the creature shattered its ice prison and came out blasting with its claws as well as its lasers. Their powers met in raw combat, with each pouring energy into the other, nullifying the power.

"Protect your mortal, witch. For if I find him first, I shall not be merciful!"

"*If* you find him first. For he is not a mere mortal, but a Maulkian Witch, with powers that shall humble you at his feet before he kills you."

The creature reviewed David's mind carefully. David had no knowledge of this. It was possible she was telling the truth. David quickly remembered that this Eve had been the target date for consummating him, and if that were the case, the witches had not yet had a chance to complete that ceremony. It was very likely Jesse had not been so initiated and thus his powers might be limited. The creature smiled.

"Bring on this male witch of yours! Let us face one another now or I shall hunt him down like the coward that he is, letting you fight his battle!"

They had moved out of earshot, and Paul began moving in closer to pick up their words. Richard looked up from loading his film.

"Hey, get back here! You're too close!"

In response to the threat to Jesse, Tamara let her lasers fly again. The huge creature was already prepared, its wing wrapped around for protection, causing the laser to ricochet wildly. Paul rose to his feet to clear the bushes that separated him from Tamara and the creature. The laser found a mark.

"No!" screamed Richard as he scrambled to his feet.

"Oh shit," breathed Paul softly, dropping his camera as he went into shock, the hole in his abdomen as big as a tea saucer. He fell back into Richard's arriving arms, and they both sank to the ground.

Richard's shout caused Tamara to turn, breaking her concentration, a break the creature didn't miss. Viciously, the creature attacked her with all of its magic. Though she was cocooned in her veil of radiance, the onslaught brought her to her knees as she struggled within herself to fight her emotions. Her heart ached for Richard and his friend. She could hear him sobbing within himself, though he made no sound as he cradled Paul, whose look of shock was still deeply etched in his face, even in death.

"How much more are you going to watch before you help?" screamed Jesse at Essadora. "Can you hate her so much that you can stand here watching her die?"

"I do not hate her—like that," stuttered Essadora, unable to take her eyes from the horrible scene.

"Then take me now!" ordered Jesse, pulling his robes open.

Richard let Paul slip gently from his arms as he numbly rose to his feet. Picking up a rock the size of a baseball, he threw it with all the experience of seventeen seasons of pitching. The unsuspecting creature took the full impact with the side of its skull; one of its horns was severed. The beast staggered slightly as it turned to face its attacker. Richard found another stone and sent it rocketing toward the creature again. This time a wing came up to deflect it harmlessly. The creature moved toward him as Richard scrambled to find a weapon. *This one is not worth wasting my power on since I still have the witch to finish,* thought the beast, *but I'm going to enjoy the feeling of this mortal's flesh ripping in my grasp!*

No sooner had their intercourse taken place when Jesse screamed out with an unearthly cry. Essadora pulled away fearfully as Jesse examined his robes as though they were burning him. He screamed over and over again as he held his head in his hands.

"It should not be so! No one has ever been affected like this!" Her own robes now fastened, Essadora clung to the ledge of the roof. They had begun the initiation on the flat area between the two spire towers of Hatisha's roof often referred to as the widow's walk. Jesse looked up from his hands, taking in large gulps of air. His entire being vibrated with uncontrollable power. Rising to his feet, he seemed to be coming out of the pain. He smiled as he turned to Essadora, his eyes completely yellow. He laughed not unlike the beast below them.

"Finally! I am free!"

"Free?" repeated Essadora, completely confused.

"Yes! Free from my mortal confines! Come! We must aid Tamara!"

"Wait—"

He spun around like a whirlwind, disappearing with a crack of thunder. Essadora moved to where Jesse had stood, searching with her open palms, trying to feel Jesse's energy. He was completely gone. She had no idea where he might be. What had happened? Why had he reacted so strangely? Tamara had said that she had created him. He was her Maulkian. It was obvious that Tamara had planned on initiating Jesse in a different way than usual. Had Essadora's little ruse worked the other night, Jesse might have gone out of control then. She realized the only thing to do now was to go to Tamara's aid herself. Perhaps together they could defeat the creature. And once it was defeated, they could combine their forces to locate Jesse, and perhaps then Tamara would know what to do.

Tamara had a choice. She could save herself by teleporting into the inner universe until she could regain her control and attack the creature anew, or she could stay to save Richard—a move that would take the last of her protection from her. Her heart and her head warred like fierce enemies. She couldn't save his friend with the creature at large, but perhaps she could buy Richard escape time; after all, there was still Essadora to carry the fight.

Richard swung the tree branch he had found at the creature with all his might, only to have the beast still its movement with a taloned fist. Yanking it free from Richard's grasp, the creature shot fire at the branch, igniting it like a match head. Its evil smile slid across its lips as it closed in on Richard. Tamara's blast seared the skin off of its back as the wings automatically arched back to protect the beast from the rest of her rays. He turned angrily, roaring with rage, sending a killing blast from its fingertips.

A witch must know her materialization point, and although she did, Essadora had clearly not counted on materializing between the creature's blast and Tamara without her shield. The startled look on Essadora's face was forever carved into Tamara's memory as she watched the face of her sister and, up until now, her enemy vanish in the disintegrating rays.

Richard's scramble for cover distracted the creature from Tamara, and the sound of cloven hooves echoed in the stillness as the beast crossed cement searching for Richard.

A warm, energizing feeling washed through Tamara, renewing her strength and doubling her power. Instantly, she knew her mother's spirit had entered her. Having chosen to give up the physical plane, Hatisha had turned herself into pure energy and, when the time was right, she had released herself within her daughter's body. Tamara felt her mother's love, her gentleness and compassion, and most importantly, her guidance to the answer of how to kill the creature.

Richard stumbled, but was back on his feet in an instant. He continued to look for a weapon—anything that would help against the hideous creature still pursuing him. If Tamara and her sisters with all their fabulous power couldn't defeat him, what good could Richard do?

Paul—dead! He still couldn't believe it. He wanted to cry, hell, he wanted to scream! They had been like brothers. He loved him. How could he possibly survive without Paul?! Without Paul, even the words sounded empty. An eerie laugh caused his stomach to knot as he turned to face his executioner.

The beast had Richard cornered in back of Hatisha's house, his tail swishing with delight as he closed in for the kill, the blood caked dry at the area of his missing horn. Twinkling radiance began to sparkle between the creature and Richard as Tamara materialized. The beast reared back in surprise, having thought it had left Tamara helpless. But what shocked the creature more, and set it immediately on guard, was the soft, provocative smile she presented to it.

"Creature of Devilin," she began softly, in a voice that caused passion to rise in David's mind and fear in the creature's, "you have proved that thou art supreme. There is no one left save for myself, and this mortal who is not worth your time. To the victor goes the spoils; I offer myself to you." Tamara crossed her hands over her heart in the sign of surrender. The beast stepped back and then forward in hesitation. His tail fluttered and danced slowly as he tried to analyze her intentions. David let the creature know that this was, indeed, a sign of surrender to the Maulkians.

"Come." She smiled sweetly, and walked away from Richard, heading to Hatisha's cellar. The creature looked at Richard only once more before following after Tamara.

She stood before the locked wooden doors that led down into the cellar and easily opened them with a wave of her hand. Lifting her robes, she gracefully descended the stairs into the interior of the altar room.

Carefully, slowly, the creature inspected its surroundings as it stepped down the stairs that led from the outside doors, its hooves echoing eerily throughout the cellar. Tamara stood before the altar, beckoning it, every candelabrum gone except for hers. The beast's wings quivered slightly at the sight of the five-pointed star drawn on the floor. Its look quickly swept to Tamara at the sound of her movements. She opened her robes and let them slowly fall around her feet, revealing her perfect body, her skin softly gleaming in the candlelight.

She stretched out her hand to him, her face more beautiful, more beseeching than any female the creature had ever seen. But with the desire that arose within came a deep, cold fear.

The beast did not know why it wanted to refuse her; somewhere in its memory was a reason he could not quite grasp. It probed David's mind for an answer, only to find that David wanted her. The beast was amused by David's longings, his urgent need to vanquish her. Then it picked up on a deeper, more intriguing emotion: revenge. David wanted to make love to Tamara, use her any way he desired, to answer the need he had built up all those years, and then he wanted to kill her.

"Here," motioned Tamara to the creature as she lay down upon the stairway of the altar. "We shall begin a new race, together."

The Devilin stood undecided for only a second longer. If David wanted the witch, then so be it. They would both revel in her. Then they would kill her.

Richard watched from the shadows of the cellar as the creature went to Tamara and lay on top of her. He couldn't believe that she had just given up. Had she done it to save him? From the dark shadows in the cellar he could not be seen, but the single candelabrum within cast giant shadows that enacted the lovemaking scene at the altar. It made him sick to his stomach, but he couldn't tear his eyes from the two of them, his jealousy making him rigid as steel. He began to think it was better to die than to have Tamara submit to this.

David couldn't believe it; he was finally where he had wanted to be for the past several years, and he couldn't even enjoy it! The creature was certainly having the time of its life—touching her, entering her, enjoying the scent of her skin—while David remained completely isolated in this small part of the creature's brain.

The Devilin was indeed enjoying this circumstance. David was raving away, harmless. This beautiful female was a cornucopia of delight. Its enemies were destroyed. A new world and a new life opened up, soon to bow at its every command and whim—what more could it want? Except, perhaps, someone to share it with. Perhaps, this female?

As the creature grunted above her, Tamara chanted silently, her eyes becoming glowing red orbs of liquid. She raised her hand over the creature, with only her index and forefinger extended and the others curled into a fist. The tips of her fingers began to glow the same eerie red as her eyes. Just as the creature climaxed, she touched the base of its brain stem through the back of its neck. Instantly, every nerve in the creature's body froze like icicles as every brain cell burned with fire. The screams of the creature reverberated through the cellar as though they had no ending or beginning. David now knew how Larry felt as he watched himself die. Her magic chanting protected Tamara from the effects of the killing touch, pulling the creature's own power from it to be used in its own destruction. The iced nerves crumbled as the brain exploded within the skull, and then the beast was nothing but a hull of ash, a returning to what it had risen from.

Tamara rose with distaste and brushed the ashes from her. Retrieving her robes, she dressed quietly, her face deeply reflecting the tiredness she felt to her soul. Richard moved toward her as she straightened herself.

"Careful not to scatter the ashes," she warned wearily. He watched the ashes as he stepped carefully around them. He then looked deeply into her eyes and opened his arms to her. She slid into them gratefully.

"I grieve for thee at the loss of your friend." Richard hugged her tighter as he tried to fight his tears. "Believe me, if I could bring him back, I would, but too much time has passed."

"I'm sorry about your mother," managed Richard quietly. Tamara looked up into his face.

"My mother is not dead, at least not in the sense you mean. She abandoned her body to become pure energy and she now dwells inside of me."

"I'm glad," he said hesitantly.

Tamara released him and turned her attention to the ashes. She spoke silently, and the ashes swirled together into the air and, like a swarm of insects, propelled out of the cellar. Once outside and hovering above Brentwood, they scattered themselves on the winds to be carried to the four corners of the earth, never to be united again.

"At first, I thought you had given up." Richard looked down at the floor guiltily. "But when your eyes started to glow, I realized it was a trick." He looked at her. "How did you kill him?"

"With his own power," she said soberly. "His own evil." She looked up at him.

"Now that you have seen what I'm capable of, are you so willing to take me in your arms?"

"For the rest of my life," he began sincerely as he took her in his arms once again, resting his face on the top of her head.

Tamara smiled, but her sadness deepened. There was so much left to do and almost no time. She released Richard and slowly climbed out of the cellar.

"What happens now?" He rubbed his face with his hands, not sure he believed all that he'd been through.

"Now," began Tamara as she moved out of the cellar and into the yard with Richard following, "I must face the greatest challenge of my life."

Richard gently took her arm and turned her to him. "What the hell do you call what just happened?" The emotions of the day were clear on his face.

"Jesse must still be saved," she whispered quietly.

"From what?"

"From himself."

Richard dropped his hand. Together they surveyed the battlefield as they returned to the front street. This section of the sleepy town of Brentwood was a shambles of smoldering buildings and scorched cornfields, but only one mortal life had been lost. Richard kneeled beside his friend. He closed Paul's eyes and arranged him peacefully. Looking up, he watched as Tamara quietly began returning Brentwood to normalcy.

The corn stood tall once again, its stalks green and yellow, even in the moonlight.

One by one the houses were restored as if this entire night had not even occurred.

All was made as before except for Hatisha's house. This now looked as though it had not been occupied for many years. The front porch was old and splintered, the flower boxes empty, save for scattered weeds, the windows dirty and cobwebbed seemed devastatingly lonely.

"Why?" asked Richard softly as he rose.

"I can restore these things, but I cannot change what has happened. We must not be here if an investigation is started, as is inevitable with the death of your friend. And unless we go, the people will not feel safe and return to their lives here."

"Where will you go?" Richard felt she was slipping away from him. He didn't want to lose her. "If we don't report Paul's death and I don't return home, then it will be a long time before anyone gets concerned. I loved him, he was the best friend I ever had—but I can do what has to be done if it means you'll stay with me."

"I know you loved your friend, just as I know that you love me. But our lives are more complicated than that. I cannot mate with anyone who is not a Maulkian Witch, no matter what my feelings. Jesse is a witch, and I care for him, and he cares deeply for me." She laughed softly, almost cynically. "Out of love, my mother gave Jesse a potion so that he would love only me for the rest of his lifetime. Now that he is a witch, his life will be as eternity. We hoped that by giving him the potion, even though we already knew his love to be true, we could keep him from wandering away like the other males of our species. Now, I am the only female he will ever want."

"Where is he?"

"His powers were exposed to him in the wrong manner. Suddenly, powers that you only dream of in your imagination are his to be used at whim. He has not had the time that I would have allowed him to adjust to my world. The power rages violently, uncontrollably within him. It was pure chance that he teleported himself into the inner universe, for now he doesn't know how to get out. This is the only thing that has saved us all from the same encounter that we have had with the beast."

"You mean he's evil now?"

"He is dangerous, but without malice. He will not want to be returned to his former self. And that will be my challenge." Suddenly, she turned to Richard and grabbed his forearms as he lifted his hands to hers, her face crowded with emotion.

"Did you mean it when you said that you would not report your friend's death?"

"Of course."

She searched his face with her dark, brooding eyes. "I will take care of your friend. Will you take care of Jesse for me? His powers will return to him slowly after I have finished. He will need guidance and understanding. Despite his age, he is still a boy. He will need a friend."

"Yes, I'll help him any way I can. But you said that you had to go away. Won't you be taking Jesse with you?" Concern replaced the sadness in his tired face.

Tamara walked a little way from him, and her look was drawn to the hill where she had made love with Jesse.

"I shall bring him out of the inner universe on that hill. That way if he resists, you will not be hurt." She looked back at him. "I shall not bother to erase your memory again. I want you to always remember me. Perhaps that will bring you closer to Jesse. You have your pictures and your cameras, do with them what you think best. You have earned your story." As her radiance enveloped her, Richard thought he saw a tear stream down her cheek. "I love thee," she said quietly as she disappeared. Richard hurried to her, but the radiance was gone. He looked to Paul, and his body was gone too. Picking up the video camera as well as the case filled with film and his thirty-five millimeter camera, he ran toward the distant hill.

The sun was just beginning to rise as Tamara drew a deep breath and looked around Brentwood and the home she had known for two centuries. She would miss this place, with its miles of cornfields—the green stalks that reached toward the blue sky with all the pride of soldiers, the yellow silk waving with the warm breezes of the Eve.

Her heart ached at the sight of the picturesque town still basking in the remnants of the Indian summer moon's glow while the stars slipped away one by one with the dawn.

But more important, she would miss Hatisha's house and the love that had dwelled within its walls. She thought of its many rooms; of how Hatisha and she would redecorate each one over and over again when boredom would overcome them. A tear momentarily filled the corner of one eye as she realized those same rooms would now be forever empty, their interiors crumbling with rot and decay.

The altar room came to mind and she fondly remembered its days of glory as its past ceremonies paraded through her mind. Not one male witch had been consummated there. She had waited so long, tried so hard to save her race, only to have the entire coven destroyed and Jesse half mad with uncontrolled power. She sighed as she hung her head. Why, why, why was it so hard to set things right and keep them on the correct course? Why must so much effort be expended just to break even?

She thought of how much Jesse had wanted to be a witch. How willing he was to give up mortal preoccupations, how she constantly had to rein his enthusiasm so that he would not rush too blindly into giving up the precious time of being a child. Jesse; young, innocent, eager, so filled with love and respect for Tamara. So willing to endure whatever she deemed necessary just to prove himself to her, just to win her love. And she did love him. Of course it had been out of necessity in the beginning, but he had won and earned her love over the past two years, now he was more than just a breeder. Sweet Jesse, she mourned to herself, how we could have continued to love one another. Our children would have been beautiful and healthy, with powers to rival any true Maulkian.

Thoughts of Richard mixed with Jesse until only Richard was left. She tried to remember him as a small child, but she could not. She had always distanced herself from the townspeople, as a result, not a single image of Richard's childhood could be conjured up. Her mind filled with their time together. He made her feel safe. How different it was to be with an equal; to not even consider powers or abilities, or the fate of the race. Richard had been the first person in Tamara's life that she could call a friend. The first genuine thing. She felt strange, she shuddered violently and sounds reached her ears as she covered her face with her hands. Her face was wet and it was then she realized she was crying. The sounds of sobbing were foreign to her and she allowed herself this one last luxury as she lost herself in the remembered feelings of Richard kissing her mouth, stroking her hair, their bodies hot with desire and passion for one another; his hands gliding to her needs; the magnificent explosion of two souls forever connected in a perpetual bond of love that time, magic or death could not extinguish.

Now drained, Tamara's dry eyes surveyed Brentwood once again. Her mother's comforting warmth was the only feeling she allowed herself as she braced herself for what would come. Forming the triangle, she began chanting as she closed her eyes in concentration. She reached out with her magic, searching the inner universe for Jesse. Finally, after several minutes, a radiance formed before her as Jesse came into view. He swung around to face her the instant he was released from the veil. His chest was heaving with an excitement he could not control. His evil, yellow eyes caused a knot in Tamara's stomach, and Jesse's fingers grasped and ungrasped as the unlimited magic within his hands raced out of control.

"Tamara! I have found you. What of the beast?"

"He is defeated, my love. Hold me." She held open her arms, her look avoiding his empty yellow eyes. Guilt ripped through her. She had done this to him. She had caused him this pain. His powers were galloping within him so recklessly, he couldn't even take a breath. Jesse laughed loudly with the same deep voice of the creature's as he took her in his arms and spun her around playfully.

"Such power, Tamara! I never realized!" He set her down and walked away from her as he looked out over the town and the ever lightening dawn. "My imagination could not compare with the reality of this." He gestured with his hands as he spoke, causing small bursts of twinkling lights to fly from his fingertips—like comets' tails, but he was referring to the magic within him and not the light show he was projecting. Tamara carefully moved toward him and he turned quickly, sensing her.

"And now, I know when you move. Before I didn't understand that it was like the waves created by throwing a stone in a pond; waves and waves of motion radiating outward."

"It will be even better when you can control the power, my love," she spoke in soothing tones as she approached him again.

"Control? When I can control?" He moved away. "I control my powers!" he retorted as he turned to her. "I shall demonstrate!" He lifted his arms, but Tamara put up her hands.

"No, I meant no disrespect, my love. Please forgive me." She moved to him and placed her hands on his. She tried not to let her relief at stopping him in time show.

"You are just afraid that I will be more powerful than you!"

His yellow eyes glared at her as she tried to calm him.

"I meant," she began, choosing her words carefully, "that as time goes by, you will have even more power, and that's when you will have to learn to control even more."

He seemed satisfied by her correction and his face took on an evil, lecherous look as he reached out with one arm and pulled her close to him.

"Now that I have been initiated, we no longer have to wait." Kissing her hard on the mouth, he moved his free hand up to the collar of her robes. "I've been waiting for two years to be able to do this." His hand parted the seam of her robes easily now that he was a witch, he no longer had to wait for her to open them.

"Wait," she whispered as she stopped his hand from traveling inside the material, "I'm in need of a hug first."

"My Tamara," his deep voice impassioned, "we now can hold each other forever!" He encircled her with his arms as she enclosed him in hers.

"I wish that were true, my Jesse." Once he was locked within her arms, she began her chanting. Tamara's veil surrounded them both, the twinkling lights began racing madly around the two. The feeling of her magic overtaking him caused him to struggle in alarm.

"What are you doing?" He pushed at her and tried to fight back with his own magic, but he couldn't control it or utter the required chants.

Dark clouds gathered over the pair as thunder rumbled across the skies. Lightning strobed its wicked fingers throughout the clouds and the wind rushed past Jesse and Tamara like a blast from the nostrils of an angry giant.

"No! No!" he cried as his voice level returned to normal. The winds slowly died down until the stillness presented an eerie epilogue to the previous maddened rush. The clouds evaporated. The lightning and thunder returned to their dark cabinet of Nature's fury until next called upon by magic or Nature itself.

Tamara's radiance slowed its unbridled gallop as the natural color returned to Jesse's eyes. Tamara's grip weakened and she began to slide down his body. Jesse pulled her up in his arms, calling to her urgently.

"Tamara? Tamara, what is it?" He went to his knees and cradled her within his arms, the cloth of their robes overlapping. She looked up at him.

"Seek out your own kind. You cannot stay here any longer. Mortals will come to expose and hurt you." Deep lines began to gather in her face. Her body began to feel lighter in his arms. Her voice became higher and softer like Hatisha's had been. "Trust only Richard, no other mortal. He will help you. He will go with you to find our kind."

"What's happening to you?" Tears of confusion rolled down his face as he watched his beautiful Tamara shriveling before his eyes. Her eyelids became dark circles, her cheeks deep hollows, the lines scurrying throughout her face as the skin lost its youthful moisture. Grayishness seemed to creep like a shadow over her features as her chest heaved with her labored breathing. Her eyes had lost their shining glow, and the lines of extreme age crept over her once beautiful face.

"It is very difficult to change another witch. It has taken all of my powers from me."

"No!" screamed Jesse.

"Seek out our kind. Take to them my ashes. I can be restored. You must go with Richard—do not stop even to say good-bye to your parents. No one must know where you have gone." She managed to lift a withered hand to his face. "Gather my ashes and I will return to you. I love thee." Her hand fell against his chest, and then the body in his arms grew weightless as it turned completely to ash.

"No! Tamara, don't leave me!" screamed Jesse as he gathered her ashes in his robes and held them to his chest.

The rising sun of the holy day shone glaringly on his tear-stained face as he rose to his knees clutching the robes tightly.

"I swear, I'll find our people. I'll bring you back, I'll find a way! I swear it!" pledged the male witch, who was now condemned to loving a woman he could never have, as Richard hurriedly climbed up the hill toward him.